The Singing Sleuth Digs Up the Past

The Singing Sleuth Digs Up the Past

D.B. Barton

Usher Press

New York   Jacksonville

The Singing Sleuth Digs Up the Past

by D.B. Barton

The Singing Sleuth Print Series:
The Singing Sleuth (2005, 2012)
The Singing Sleuth Returns (2007, 2014)
The Singing Sleuth Goes Home (2009, 2017)
The Singing Sleuth Crosses the Pond (2011, 2021)
The Singing Sleuth Does Vegas (2013)
The Singing Sleuth Takes a Bow (2016)
The Singing Sleuth Meets His Matches (2020)
The Singing Sleuth Runs a B&B (2022)
The Singing Sleuth Finds a Leaf (2023)
The Singing Sleuth Digs Up the Past (2024)
The Singing Sleuth Gets Snowed Under (2025)

The complete series can be ordered directly from
www.singingsleuth.com.

Printed in the United States of America

To amateur
detectives and archaeologists:

You both share a desire
to make the unknown known!

Contents

Prologue 1

Chapter 1: "Join Together" 9

Chapter 2: "Everybody Wants to Rule the World" 17

Chapter 3: "Behind Blue Eyes" 24

Chapter 4: "Another One Bites the Dust" 34

Chapter 5: "Kokomo" 45

Chapter 6: "The Caves of Altamira" 54

Chapter 7: "Lemon Tree" 62

Chapter 8: "On and On" 71

Chapter 9: "Addicted to Love" 83

Chapter 10: "Money, Money, Money" 91

Chapter 11: "Panama" 98

Chapter 12: "Live to Tell" 109

Chapter 13: "Bungle in the Jungle" 117

Chapter 14: "Honesty" 127

Chapter 15: "Spinning Wheel" 138

Chapter 16: "Witchcraft" 148

Chapter 17: "Three Little Birds" 157

Chapter 18: "My Funny Valentine" 165

Epilogue 175

Answers to Archaeology Quiz 181

Copyright Acknowledgements 185

Pegasus Itinerary

Eleven-Day Panama Canal Cruise
Fort Lauderdale to Fort Lauderdale

Date	Day	Port of Call	Arrival	Departure
4-Feb	Sun	Fort Lauderdale, Florida		4:00 PM
5-Feb	Mon	Coral Cay, Bahamas	8:00 AM	3:00 PM
6-Feb	Tue	*At Sea*		
7-Feb	Wed	Oranjestad, Aruba	1:00 PM	10:30 PM
8-Feb	Thu	Willemstad, Curaçao	7:00 AM	4:00 PM
9-Feb	Fri	*At Sea*		
10-Feb	Sat	Cartagena, Columbia	7:00 AM	2:00 PM
11-Feb	Sun	Enter Panama Canal	5:00 AM	
11-Feb	Sun	Gatun Lake	9:00 AM	10:30 PM
11-Feb	Sun	Exit Panama Canal		1:00 PM
11-Feb	Sun	Colon, Panama	3:00 PM	8:00 PM
12-Feb	Mon	Puerto Limon, Costa Rica	6:30 AM	3:30 PM
13-Feb	Tue	*At Sea*		
14-Feb	Wed	*At Sea*		
15-Feb	Thu	Fort Lauderdale, Florida	7:00 AM	

PROLOGUE

▼

Saturday Afternoon
3rd of February
4:57 PM EST

Alec was seated at his office desk when a knock sounded at the door. After calling, "Come in," his jaw fell a half inch. Standing in the entranceway was the captain of the ship.

Quickly, Alec rose to his feet to clear the clutter from his desk. The new captain of the Pegasus, Charles Stewart, was intimidating. Despite being of average height and weight, he seemed to suck all the oxygen from the room.

Nearly breathless, Alec stammered, "Would you like to take a seat?"

Alec glanced at the chair in front of the desk and was relieved to see that there were no papers on it.

Captain Stewart inclined his bald head and took the offered seat. Using perfect Oxford English, which he employed while speaking to his officers, the captain remarked, "Tomorrow, members of the Florida Archaeology Organization are going to board the ship. I understand you've been working with the cruise director to accommodate them."

Not certain where Stewart was going with the statement, Alec nodded his head. As controller on the Pegasus, he monitored how much money passengers spent on extra shipboard fees and services during their cruise. He set up monetary goals for every department on the ship. That included the bars, specialty restaurants, shops, internet/photograph packages, casino, spa, and gym.

Though he didn't have much to do with group reservations or their events, he had recently ordered books on archaeology, pirates of the Caribbean, and the building of the Panama Canal. From his brief conversation with Faith Rossi, the cruise director, Alec was also aware that she had arranged for the archaeologists to conduct a few passenger lectures.

Captain Stewart didn't waste time and announced with a slight smile, "I happen to be an amateur archaeologist. I took classes at university and volunteered on several digs in the Middle East and Africa. I want you to oversee the archeologists' activities and make sure they go without a hitch. I plan to take part in several of their events."

With that said, the captain rose from the chair and headed to the door. Before departing, he turned to Alec and said, "I've been told that you're the man to see if any *unusual* problems crop up."

Alec wasn't surprised that Stewart had heard about his abilities. In the past, Alec had been called upon to investigate murders on Flagship Cruise Line ships and it's resort in Las Vegas.

To solve those cases, Alec used song lyrics to describe his suspects, unravel motives, and decipher clues. When he needed to have a "good think," he smoked his trusty pipe. Paige, Alec's lovely wife, was especially helpful in interviewing persons of interest and following leads.

Alec's musings were interrupted when the assistant controller rushed into the room and asked, "Did I just see our captain leave your office? What did he want?"

Regina Hill was a rather short and plump woman. Despite being in her early seventies, she had an ageless quality and an ability to see through people. She was the perfect person to assist Alec in both his accounting and sleuthing duties.

While Regina was tucking a stray strand of gray hair into her tidy bun, Alec replied, "Stewart wants me to keep an eye on some archaeologists who are going to board the ship tomorrow. It's possible he heard something negative about the group."

"Good luck on that," Regina laughed. "You seem to attract killers like a bee to honey. You're not called 'The Singing Sleuth' for nothing."

Over the next hour, Alec put aside his accounting work to look into the Florida Archaeology Organization. Its website contained information about the group's objectives and its membership requirements. On the site, there was a place to apply for awards and give donations. Under officers, there were several names listed with photographs. Included was the president, secretary, treasurer, and former president.

The current president of the FAO, Annette Perkins, looked like a bulldog. She had short, salt and pepper hair, sagging jowls, a wrinkled brow, and a pug nose. Her expression said, "Don't mess with me."

After Alec uttered a sound in response to her photo, Regina remarked, "That bad?"

Laughing, Alec replied, "It's getting late. I'm going to see what more info Faith may have on the group."

Regina sighed, "Go ahead. I'll lock up."

Thankful he had such a dependable assistant, Alec headed over to the cruise director's office.

Fortunately, Faith was seated at her desk and had the names and cabin numbers of the twenty-two FAO members booked on the cruise. Alec glanced at the list. Annette Perkins, the president of the organization, was the first name on it. The other names meant nothing to him, and their cabins were scattered all over the ship.

From a pile of papers on her desk, the cruise director handed Alec a flyer listing the organization's upcoming events. It read,

Scheduled Activities for Florida Archaeologists

<u>Sunday, 4th of February</u>
Depart, *Fort Lauderdale, Florida: 4:00pm*
Sail-Away Party, *Explorer's Club: 5:00pm to 6:00pm*

<u>Monday, 5th of February</u>
Shore Excursions, *Coral Cay, Bahamas: 7:30am to 2:30pm*
Informal Beach Luncheon, *Coral Cay, Bahamas: 12:00pm to 1:30pm*
Evening Get Together, *Constellation Lounge: 8:00pm to 10:00pm*

<u>Tuesday, 6th of February (At Sea)</u>
FAO Morning Meeting, *Hudson Room: 10:00am to 11:00am*
Panama Canal Film, *Starlight Lounge: 1:00pm to 2:00pm*
First Archaeology Talk, *Starlight Lounge: 2:00pm to 3:00pm*
Captain's Gala Welcome Party, *Starlight Lounge: 7:00pm*

<u>Wednesday, 7th of February</u>
Archaeology Trivia, *Explorer's Club: 10:00am to 11:00am*
Shore Excursions, *Oranjestad, Aruba: 1:00pm to 10:30pm*

<u>Thursday, 8th of February</u>
Shore Excursions, *Willemstad, Curaçao: 7:00am to 3:30pm*
FAO Pre Dinner Drinks, *Constellation Lounge: 6:00pm*
FAO Dinner Party, *Rainbow Grill: 7:00pm*

<u>Friday, 9th of February (At Sea)</u>
FAO Morning Meeting, *Hudson Room: 10:00am to 11:00am*
Second Archaeology Talk, *Starlight Lounge: 2:00pm to 3:00pm*

<u>Saturday, 10th of February</u>
Shore Excursions, *Cartagena, Columbia: 7:00am to 2:00pm*
FAO Afternoon Meeting, *Churchill Room: 2:30pm to 3:30pm*

<u>Sunday, 11th of February</u>
Scenic Viewing, *Panama Canal, Bow (Deck 7): 6:30am*
Shore Excursions Depart, Gatun Lake, Panama: *9:00am to10:30am*
Ship Reverses and Exits, *Panama Canal: 1:00pm*
Shore Excursions Return, *Colon, Panama: 3:00pm to 10:00pm*

<u>Monday, 12th of February</u>
Shore Excursions, *Puerto Limon, Costa Rica: 6:30am to 3:30pm*
FAO Afternoon Meeting, *Churchill Room: 3:30pm to 4:30pm*

<u>Tuesday, 13th of February (At Sea)</u>
Third Archaeology Talk, *Starlight Lounge: 2:00pm to 3:00pm*
Archaeology Trivia, *Explorer's Club: 8:00pm to 9:00pm*

<u>Wednesday, 14th of February (At Sea)</u>
FAO Farewell Cocktail Party, *Explorer's Club: 6:00pm to 7:00pm*

<u>Thursday, 15th of November</u>
Arrive, *Fort Lauderdale, Florida: 7:00am*

Alec noted that the group planned to hold several private meetings as well as three public talks with cruise passengers. Faith didn't think the archaeologists were going to be any trouble and said, "They're probably dry as dust."

After thanking Faith, Alec tucked the papers into his pocket and set off for his suite. Although most officers were given standard-sized quarters on the Dolphin Deck of the Pegasus, Alec and Paige had an oversized cabin, steps from his office.

The DunBarton's quarters contained a sitting area large enough to accommodate six people. Between their living room and modest kitchenette was a slim counter and two stools that served as a dining area. The couple's bedroom and bathroom were somewhat hidden from the rest of their lodgings by a few pieces of well-placed furniture.

Like many passenger cabins on the Lower Promenade Deck, the cabins had two doors—one leading to the inside corridor and the other to the promenade deck. The Pegasus advertised these accommodations as Prom Cabins.

Alec was freshening up when Paige entered their suite. Upon hearing her, he stepped out of the bathroom to greet her.

Wearily, Paige slipped off her medium-sized heels, complaining, "I'm exhausted! I just spent an hour with a difficult passenger who plans to take back-to-back cruises with her dog and cat. After much discussion, she agreed to leave her pets at home with her middle-aged daughter."

Alec kissed the top of her head and suggested, "Let's have a quiet dinner tonight. While you run your nightly bath, I'll pick up dinner from the Lido Buffet."

Not wasting a minute, Paige removed her uniform and turned on the bathtub's tap. As she was adding bath gel to the cascading water, Alec asked, "What can I get you?"

Upon hearing her choices in order of preference, Alec saluted, "I'll be back soon, Lass. Enjoy your bath."

The Lido Buffet was crowded with passengers trying to relish their last night of the cruise. For the ship's staff, it meant one voyage was ending and another beginning.

Alec had to wait several minutes to pick up a bowl of pasta with butter and cheese for Paige and a cheeseburger and fries for himself. With a loaded tray, Alec returned to his cabin to find his wife wrapped up in a terrycloth robe and sitting up in bed.

As she rose to help him with the dinner entrees, Paige gazed at Alec and muttered, "You have a secret, don't you? I can tell by the sparkle in your eyes. Come clean."

Alec winked. "Captain Stewart stopped by my office this afternoon. A group of archaeologists are boarding the ship tomorrow, and he wants me to make sure they settle in nicely."

Paige nearly dropped her bowl of spaghetti as she transferred it from the tray to the kitchen counter and said in a worried tone, "Does he expect trouble?"

Noting her pinched features, Alec put her concerns to rest and replied, "Not at all. Apparently, our captain is an amateur archaeologist. I think he merely wants to impress the group."

Paige wasn't so sure and remarked, "No one had better get murdered!"

To remove her doubts, Alec showed her the FAO's schedule of events. After seeing the rather mundane activities, she conceded, "I guess it will be alright."

CHAPTER ONE

▼

"Join Together"
Words & Music by Pete Townshend
Genre: Classic Rock, Released: June 1972

Sunday Afternoon—4th of February

Alec and Paige spent the morning helping crew members disembark the passengers. There were always a few who needed more attention than others. Some with early flights or a long drive back home often required an extra hand to haul three or more pieces of luggage from their cabin to the terminal.

The majority of passengers were in public areas on the Pegasus waiting for their debarkation numbers to be announced. Dutifully, those guests had left their suitcases outside their cabins the night before. Among them, there were always a few people who packed everything, including the clothes they planned to wear the following day.

The last group of passengers could be found at the Lido Buffet, enjoying a leisurely breakfast and in no rush to leave the ship. They were bread-and-butter guests who often sailed on the cruise line. They had been retired for many years and usually had another trip planned in three to four months' time.

While waiting for the new crop of passengers to board, Alec and Paige fit in a quick lunch and then headed to Paige's cruise consultant desk. It was a stone's throw from the Front Desk, where passengers congregated to ask the ship's receptionists to change their cabins or answer questions about the sailing.

Paige's exotic cruise brochures frequently caught the eye of bored husbands or wives. It was the ideal time for guests to schedule appointments with her. After giving his wife a goodbye kiss, Alec took the atrium steps down to his office.

Regina was working on a revenue report. She looked up from her computer when Alec entered the room and moaned "I hope the Pegasus earns more on this upcoming voyage. On the last one, we barely met Flagship Cruise Line's projections."

Alec replied, "It does get monotonous. Those archaeologists may improve our shipboard sales. Did all the merchandise we ordered come in?"

Regina nodded. "I went by The Shops earlier. The sales staff had just finished setting up the display. One of the pirate books caught my eye. I think my youngest grandson may like it."

Alec smiled. "You alone can improve our numbers!"

Eager to find out more about the archaeologists, Alec turned on his computer and returned to the FAO site. With the list of its twenty-two members beside him, Alec looked up Annette Perkins and read her short bio with interest. Other than being the organization's president, he learned she was a CRM.

Having no idea what those initials stood for, Alec googled the abbreviations and discovered it stood for Cultural Resource Manager. Perkins worked for a private company and was responsible for surveying property to make certain that new roads or buildings were not going to destroy a historic site. The internet said that 90% of archaeology work done in the United States fell under cultural resource management.

Wondering whether any builders had issues with her job, Alec looked at the remaining twenty-one members on the list. He noted that the treasurer and former president were also going to be on the cruise. The secretary of the organization was not among them.

The treasurer of the FAO was a woman by the name of Emily Irving. From her photograph, Alec judged her to be middle aged. She had an angelic face and expressive brown eyes. Her field of study was biblical archaeology.

The photo of the former president, Aaron Sloane, was taken from a distance. Behind him was a large boat that looked very expensive. The fellow looked like a show off, used to flaunting his latest acquisitions. Under his writeup, it mentioned that he specialized in underwater excavations and had unearthed treasures and artifacts from Spanish Main ships.

After familiarizing himself with the FAO officers, Alec looked over the cabin assignments. A few people on the list shared the same last name, and Alec assumed they were married or related to each other. Alec was not surprised to see men and women with different surnames assigned to the same cabin. It was less expensive for a single guest to share a room.

In order to have private quarters, passengers had to pay a single supplement. Among those were Annette Perkins, Victor Bristow, and Aaron Sloane. Alec noted that Jennifer Bristow was rooming with Emily Irving. Hoping that Jennifer was either Victor's daughter or sister, and not an estranged wife, Alec continued his search.

Alec's last task was to look up individual members on the internet. Several were mentioned in archeological journals and a few had no online presence. One newspaper had an article about Michael Donovan, an underwater archaeologist, who worked for Aaron Sloane and had discovered a pirate ship from the 1500s. He was sharing his cabin with a Marshall Weissman.

There was a great deal on Aaron Sloane and his explorations. More interesting than his findings was a separate article about Sloane's wife, Lena. She died from a snake bite while on a dig in Panama. The death of Lena Sloane occurred five years earlier and was ruled a misadventure by Panamanian officials. At the time of her accident, she was with her husband and a group of university students studying archaeology.

The piece also stated that venom from a snake bite caused Sloane's internal organs to shut down. She passed away shortly after reaching a hospital in Panama City. The details were quite gory and Alec realized that archaeology could be dangerous and not for the timid.

At 4:00 PM, the ship's whistles signaled its attention to sail along with an announcement from the cruise director advising passengers, who had not done so, to go to their muster station and give their name to the crewmember on duty. Any individual that refused could be put ashore.

Curious about his new captain, Alec typed the name, Charles Stewart, into the computer's search bar. From public and shipboard sources, Alec gleaned that the captain was in his early sixties, born in Mirfield, England, with FCL twenty-six years, and divorced. His hobbies and interests included archeology, pickleball, and fencing.

Alec had no trouble visualizing Stewart with a sword in his hand. Despite being totally bald, the captain made a dashing figure. His piercing hazel eyes had a way of looking past a person's façade.

While Alec was finishing up his research, Regina reminded him that he and Paige had promised to join her and Dr. Abbot for dinner at seven. Noting that it was four thirty and the FAO were scheduled to have a Welcome Aboard Cocktail Party at the Explorer's Club at 5:00 o'clock. Alec hurried toward the office door.

Before exiting, he turned to his assistant and relayed, "I'm going to meet the FAO members in the flesh. I'll give you an update at dinner!"

Alec took the atrium staircase one-level up to Paige's Future Cruise Desk. She was in the midst of scheduling an appointment with two passengers the following day. After the couple departed, she looked at her husband with an amused expression and said, "You look like a man on a mission."

Alec smiled. "I am, indeed. I want you to join me for drinks at the Explorer's Club. The Florida Archaeology Organization is meeting there for a Sail-Away Party between five and six."

Concerned, they might be overstepping, Paige voiced, "Is it okay for us to crash their soiree?"

Alec cajoled, "You don't want to disobey the captain's orders, do you?" With that said, Paige acquiesced and they made their way to the lounge.

Although Alec and Paige arrived minutes early, the party was in full swing. There were a number of people talking in small groups, and a DJ was stationed in the corner of the room playing rock music.

The Explore's Club was the perfect place for the archaeologists to gather. The lounge was decorated with nautical instruments and other maritime artifacts from Flagship Cruise Line's earliest vessels.

A short man with beady blue eyes, bristly hair, and an unshaven chin approached the pair. Alec gazed at him for a moment and realized he was Aaron Sloane. Before Alec could say anything, the fellow remarked rudely, "This is a private function."

Sizing him up, Alec replied, "We're with the ship. My wife and I have been asked by Captain Stewart to make sure everything goes smoothly at your function. He's an amateur archaeologist and plans to attend some of your events. I believe he's cleared it with your group's president."

Not sure he did, Alec looked around the room and said, "Perhaps I should speak to Annette Perkins."

The man looked over to where the FAO president was standing and relented, "I guess it's okay for you to be here. My name is Aaron Sloane. I served as the organization's president before handing the reins to Annette."

Perkins must have noticed the threesome and came over seconds later. She appeared even more like a bulldog in the flesh and her voice was hoarse when she spoke. A bit more courteous than Sloane, she introduced herself first and invited, "Please feel free to join us any time. Your captain contacted me prior to this cruise and we're at his disposal."

At that moment, the disc jockey played a song by The Who. Before he could stop himself, Alec sang out,

When you hear this sound a-comin'
Hear the drummer drumming
Won't you join together with the band
We don't move in any 'ticular direction
And we don't make no collections
Won't you join together with the band

Do you really think I care
What you eat or what you wear
Won't you join together with the band
There's a million ways to laugh
Every one's a path
Won't you join together with the band

Everybody join together
Won't you join together
Come on and join together with the band
We need to join together
Won't you join together
Come on and join together with the band

You don't have to play
You can follow or lead the way
Won't you join together with the band
We don't know where we're going
But the season's right for knowing
Won't you join together with the band

It's the singer not the song
That makes the music move along
Won't you join together with the band
This is the biggest band you'll find
It's as deep as it is wide
Won't you join together with the band

Everybody join together

Won't you join together
Come on and join together with the band
We need to join together
Won't you join together
Come on and join together with the band

Like most people who were treated to Alec's launch into song, Annette laughed heartily and suddenly became less reserved. She agreed that the lyrics to the song and the Explorer's Club was a particularly apt place for their little "band of explorers."

Sloane, on the other hand, looked at Alec as though he had two heads. When he walked away. Annette stared at his departing figure with annoyance and then invited Alec and Paige to help themselves to drinks and appetizers.

Over the next hour, Alec and Paige mingled with several people. Among them was Victor Bristow. He was taller than Aaron and sported a deadpan expression. His aloofness disappeared when he introduced his daughter, Jennifer, to the DunBartons.

Jennifer Bristow was a beauty with long brown hair and an infectious smile. Her enthusiasm about being on the cruise made others feel excited about the places they were to visit. Proudly, Victor explained that Jennifer was employed by the Florida Museum of History in Tallahassee.

Jennifer responded by saying, "My dad is no slouch either. He works for the state government as well and was instrumental in unearthing some incredible finds when the Mission San Luis de Apalachee was reconstructed. The site was a Spanish Franciscan mission, built in 1656. For many years, the Spanish and native American Apalachees lived side by side in relative harmony."

Paige was surprised and admitted, "Alec and I know so little about Floridian history despite having our home port of call in Fort Lauderdale. We heard that FAO members are going to conduct a few lectures during the cruise."

Victor agreed. "We haven't decided upon the topics yet, but they're sure to be interesting."

Hearing raised voices over the music, Alec and Paige shifted their attention to a couple that was shouting at each other. Sloane was obviously angry with Emily, the FAO's treasurer.

In response, Victor Bristow explained, "Not all our members get along well. Sloane can be difficult and derisive. He and Emily Irving look at archaeology in totally different ways. Emily is a biblical archaeologist and Sloane thinks she's delusional, trying to prove that biblical figures from the Old Testament really existed."

Jennifer then whispered to her dad, "Sometimes, Sloane gives me the creeps."

Victor gave the man a look that could kill.

Alec whistled and said to Paige, "We might be in for an exciting cruise!"

CHAPTER TWO

▼

"Everybody Wants to Rule the World"
Words & Music by Ian Stanley,
Roland Orzabal, and Chris Hughes
Genre: New Age Rock, Released: March 1985

__Monday Morning—5th of February__

After spending the previous evening at the party and dining with Dr. Douglas Abbot and Regina, the DunBartons decided to sleep in an extra hour. Unfortunately, the pair could not linger in bed.

At nine o'clock, Paige set off for her office and, minutes later, Alec hopped into the shower, dressed, and hurried to sickbay on the Dolphin Deck. He had promised to help Douglas transfer some medical supplies to the Coral Cay infirmary on Flagship Cruise Line's private island.

Douglas was waiting with an impatient expression when Alec arrived and said, "I don't suppose you've had breakfast yet."

Alec grinned, "No, I haven't. Are you going to offer me something?"

The doctor grunted. "I'll finish gathering up the last few items myself. Get a bite from the Officer's Lounge. But, make it quick."

Alec saluted, "Yes, Sir. I'll be back in moments, Sir."

Douglas laughed and waved him away. "Don't give me any lip, Sergeant!"

The two men, laden with insulated bags and several boxes, headed up to the Main Deck on the ship to take a tender to the island's dock. There were several passengers in line to take the small boat. On Coral Cay, guests were invited to take part in activities that included nature walks, glass bottom boat rides, kayaking, biking, and horseback riding.

Less active passengers could reserve a costly private cabana with a butler or an inexpensive sunshade with two lounge chairs. For those who didn't plan ahead, there was plenty of white sand to spread their towels on.

At noon, a buffet barbeque luncheon was served. Among the entrees were a variety of side dishes, grilled meat and chicken, soft drinks, and desserts. The line for ice cream cones was always long.

The ride to the island took about ten minutes. Alec enjoyed the salty sea air and the breeze in his hair. Earlier in the morning, the skies were overcast. Now, the sun was breaking through the clouds, and it promised to be a beautiful day.

Douglas and Alec stepped off the tender with the rest of the passengers. Instead of taking the walkway to the beach and water sports area, the two men split off the path for the infirmary. A nurse on duty greeted them with a smile and relayed, "It's been quiet, so far. I expect it will get busier as the weather improves."

Alec didn't stay long. Since he had no pressing concerns back at the office and Regina was more than capable of holding down the fort, Alec decided to walk around the small island and see whether any of the FAO members were up and about.

At the FAO party, Alec had tried to memorize the faces of its members. Most of them were quite talkative and excited about visiting the port of calls on the cruise. Others were eager to tell Alec and Paige about artifacts they had unearthed on various digs.

Since Alec didn't recognize anyone on the beach, he strolled over to the Beachcomber Bar. Seated at a balcony table was Aaron Sloane. He was with a well-tanned man and an unattractive fellow with zinc oxide ointment on his nose. Alec had seen the two at the party but didn't get a chance to speak to them.

Not wasting the opportunity, Alec ordered a soft drink and asked if he could join the threesome. Speaking for Sloane, the zinc oxide guy, pulled out a spare chair and invited Alec to sit. He introduced himself, "I'm Marshall Weissman, the technological expert of our team."

Sloane gave Weissman a hard stare that said, "I didn't give you permission to talk."

Marshall didn't seem to care and continued, "I saw you and your wife at that cocktail party. Are you archaeologists? What's your specialty?"

When he took a breath, Alec replied, "My wife Paige and I noticed you, too and were curious about the kind of work you do."

Weissman explained, "I'm the nerd of the group. We, that's Mr. Sloane, Michael, and I work together on exploring the ocean's depths for buried ships from the sixteenth and seventeenth centuries." Kidding around, he added, "Arrgh matey. You can say we look for pirate treasure and plunder."

Sloane gave Marshall another nasty look when Michael intervened, "My name is Michael Donovan. I'm an underwater archaeologist. I just go where I'm told and search the sea beds for anomalies "

Alec nodded. "I read about your team. I looked you up on the internet yesterday when I learned you were going to be on this cruise. You've been all over the world and have found some amazing things."

Sloane agreed. "We've been very fortunate. I must say Marshall is a whiz at locating the right sites for us to explore."

Instead of enjoying the compliment, Marshall went into a longwinded description of his remote sensing devices, including infrared photography, proton magnetometers, multispectral satellite imagery, geographic information systems, ground penetrating radar, fluxgate gradiometers, and electrical resistivity.

Alec gave up trying to understand what each device did and waited for Marshall to finish. The three men made an unusual team. Sloane was controlling and demanding, Donovan unassuming and shy, and Weissman, a self-centered nerd.

Noting the time, Alec finished his soda and asked whether they planned to have lunch with the other members of their group. Sloane didn't seem too eager to rub shoulders with his fellow archaeologists, but the other two readily agreed they would walk over to the designated area closer to lunchtime.

Soon after, Alec departed and set off for the picnic area. As he neared the island's food buffet, the scent of barbequed meats assailed Alec's nostrils, and he realized that the few mini-Danishes he'd ingested for breakfast was doing nothing to control his hunger.

The picnic tables were located in airy huts and the foliage around the structures gave its diners a sense of privacy. The ship's guests often had issues finding their table after returning with a second helping. As a result, the cruise line numbered the eating areas.

Hut seven with five tables was assigned to the FAO members. There was a poster specifying that a private party was to take place. Annette Perkins was with Emily Irving, the woman who had gotten in an argument with Aaron Sloane.

When he approached them, Annette beckoned Alec over and said. "I don't know whether you met Emily Irving yet. She's our treasurer and has helped me plan many of our events."

Speaking to Emily, she added, "The captain wants us to contact Mr. DunBarton if any issues arise."

While the women chatted about the logistics, Alec decided that Emily Irving was even more lovely close up. She was petite and her voice, like her countenance, was soft and feminine.

Wanting to know more about her, Alec said, "I understand you're a biblical archaeologist. What does that entail?"

Pleasantly, Emily replied, "I look for evidence to support historical records in the Bible. When I'm not in the field, I teach several courses at Trinity Southeast University. It's a Christian college in Fort Lauderdale."

As she was finishing her sentence, Captain Stewart arrived. Emily gave him a brilliant smile and said, "Charles was one of my best students."

A slight blush crossed the captain's pale face. It disappeared after Stewart ordered Alec, "Walk with me."

Alec had no idea what he planned to say to him and was relieved when he announced, "I'm glad you're keeping an eye on the FAO members. I'm particularly concerned about Aaron Sloane. Have you made his acquaintance yet?"

In response to Alec's nod, the captain resumed, "That man is a tyrant and would love to rule the world."

With that said, Stewart departed, and Alec launched into song,

Welcome to your life
There's no turning back
Even while we sleep
We will find you

Acting on your best behavior
Turn your back on Mother Nature
Everybody wants to rule the world

It's my own desire
It's my own remorse
Help me to decide
Help me make the most of freedom
And of pleasure
Nothing ever lasts forever

Everybody wants to rule the world
There's a room where the light won't find you
Holding hands while the walls come tumbling down
When they do, I'll be right behind you
So glad we've almost made it
So sad we had to fade it
Everybody wants to rule the world
Everybody wants to rule the world
Everybody wants to rule the world

The FAO luncheon went smoothly. Aaron Sloane appeared to be on his best behavior and the others got along fine. Emily Irving was particularly lively, chatting with everyone about her latest discoveries.

Alec also noticed that Jennifer Bristow had caught the eye of Michael Donovan. Victor, Jen's father, did not look happy about it. Out of all the members, Alec found Marshall Weissman the most interesting. The fellow followed the archaeologists around like a puppy dog. When he received their attention, his eyes lit up and you could picture him wagging his nonexistent tail.

Alec stayed long enough to pick up lunch and mention to Annette Perkins that he planned to attend the FAO's get together in the Constellation Lounge. Annette, expressing some reluctance, explained, "It might be boring for you. We're planning to discuss the contents of our first lecture. We haven't decided upon a topic yet or the person to lead the talk."

After assuring her that he and Paige would find it interesting, she acquiesced and added, "We're going to start at 8:00 PM."

On his return to the ship, Alec headed over to the future cruise desk. Paige was alone and looked up at Alec expectantly. Winking, she stated, "I just met a lovely couple that booked an upcoming cruise to the Mediterranean. They're members of that archaeological group. The wife was chatty and had plenty to say about her fellow members."

Taking a seat in front of her desk, Alec urged her to go on.

Paige resumed, "The woman told me that Annette Perkins treats many of the members with distain and dotes upon others. Despite her flaws, the couple really disliked Aaron Sloane when he was president. He's been known to sell valuable finds to private individuals as opposed to donating them to museums for the public to enjoy. The sale of artifacts is regarded as looting and a big no-no among archaeologists."

Alec moved closer to his wife as she continued, "The couple also told me that Lena Sloane, Aaron's wife, was a real character. She was bitten by a snake and died horribly. Even though she was a bona fide member of the FAO, many in the group considered her a celebrity archaeologist. Her television programs and videos were filmed on location and from active archaeological sites all over the world."

Looking over her shoulder to make sure no one could hear her, Paige added, "Lena had loose morals and slept around with a few men in the FAO. Among them was Victor Bristow and some other member. They're both on this cruise."

Alec grinned. "I guess you won't be disappointed if we join them in the Constellation Lounge tonight."

Paige agreed, "No, but you'd better buy me a drink or two."

CHAPTER THREE

▼

"Behind Blue Eyes"
Words & Music by Pete Townshend
Genre: Hard Rock, Released: June 1971

Monday Evening—5th of February

Paige and Alec arrived a few minutes past eight. There were about fifteen members seated in the corner of the room. The lounge was one of Alec's favorite places to relax. The Constellation Lounge was located on the Observation Deck and surrounded by floor-to-ceiling bay windows. During the day, passengers were treated to incredible views of the ocean and, at night, small bright lights in the domed ceiling sparkled in the configuration of constellations.

The archaeologists seemed immune to the magical dancing of the stars and were fully attuned to what Annette Perkins was saying. The DunBartons sat down at a table near the FAO president.

Annette was in the midst of asking the group what they wanted to discuss at their first public lecture on Tuesday. Paige pointed out the couple she spoke to earlier in the day. They just nodded in agreement with everything Annette said.

Victor Bristow was the most adamant and said, "I think we should begin our lecture series with the basics, such as the archaeological process, how to prepare a dig site, ways to date a find, and what artifacts tell people about our past."

Aaron nearly stopped him midsentence but closed his mouth when Annette held up her hand. As soon as Victor finished, Sloane complained, "You're going to put the whole ship to sleep. I want to discuss what my team discovered in the Caribbean. Afterall, we're going to visit Panama where many of the Spanish treasure ships were scuttled."

Annette replied, "That will be a better topic for our second talk. Who agrees?"

Most of the hands went up and she pronounced, "That's settled. At Friday's lecture, we'll include historic background relating to the colonization of the Americas by the Spanish, French, Dutch, and British in the sixteenth and seventeenth centuries. Afterward, Aaron, you'll have a perfect opportunity to bring up famous clashes at sea and what you and your team unearthed from the ocean floor."

Sloane readily agreed and added, "I have some fantastic slides of the artifacts we found."

Perkins replied, "I'll make sure the cruise director sets up the relevant equipment for your presentation."

She continued, "I agree with Victor that out first discussion should include the basics. To make it more palatable to the general public, we can have a panel of members speak and include photos of dig sites and the equipment we use to conduct one. Passengers who want more information about what we do can be given an opportunity to ask questions at the end of the talk. Can we vote upon my second proposal?"

When everyone responded to the president, Alec summoned over the bartender and ordered Paige a gin and tonic, and a neat Glenlivet for himself. While waiting for the drinks to be served, Alec tried to decipher the voices, all asking who was going to be included on the panel.

After trying to silence them, Annette raised her voice. "Enough! I've heard you. Victor, I'd like you to define archaeology and give the audience a printed timeline that encompasses human development from the beginning to the present."

Victor acknowledged that he had "just the thing," and suggested, "My daughter, as a museum curator, can show a power point of artifacts that were found during major periods."

Perkins agreed and then pointed to Marshall Weissman. "Can you discuss some of our dating methods?"

Marshall went into a long-winded response promising to be succinct and to refrain from techno babble. When she told him to keep his portion of the talk to about ten minutes, he gulped and said he would try.

Emily Irving spoke next and asked if she would be allowed to talk about biblical archaeology at another time. After getting a consensus from the other members, Perkins promised that she, along with other archaeologists, would get an opportunity to discuss their individual fields of study.

In response, Sloane immediately rose and shouted, "The public will think we're clowns!"

Most of the members sat quietly while he retorted, "Irving believes that God created the entire universe six days and all life was put on earth fully formed. She'll make us a laughing stock."

With complete calmness, Emily replied, "You know very well, I believe the universe is about 14 billion years old and the Big Bang occurred on day one of Genesis. Further, I subscribe to the Day-Age Theory, which states that the first six days of Genesis were not literal twenty-four-hour days, but rather an indefinite period of time that coincided with the geographical transformations that took place on earth.

"There's no need for you to deride biblical archaeology. We're in agreement as to the age of the earth and that within species, there were evolutionary changes. Unlike you, however, I believe in God and have faith in a power greater than ourselves."

Before Sloane could argue, Perkins announced, "I want everyone to be civil to each other. Biblical archeology and other historic deductions should be presented at our third talk. Please let me know what you'd like to discuss over the next few days. The public may find the topic of early man, cannibalism in the U.S. Southeast, and/or Asian hobbits interesting. It's important for them to know we don't have all the answers and must continually reassess our conclusions."

With that said, the group broke into smaller groups—some debating archaeological matters and others conversing about the cruise. While at the bar to pick up a bowl of peanuts, Alec sidled up to Sloane who was ordering a bourbon on ice.

Although he had a permanent sneer on his face, Alec said, "I find your views interesting. Would you like to join my wife and me?" Sloane nodded in response and followed Alec to where Paige was seated."

Alec realized that Paige had read his mind when she remarked, "I can see that archaeologists don't always agree."

Sloane took the bait and confessed, "I know I shouldn't let Emily rattle me. She has a right to her own opinions even though so little of it can be proven. She also went to college with my wife and had remained friendly with Lena until her death. I've often wondered how much my wife had shared with Emily about me."

Alec was surprised by his vulnerable admission and said, "I understand your wife died about five years ago."

Sloane shook his head in acknowledgement. "I haven't been back to Panama since it happened. Lena and a film crew had planned to do a piece on a pre-Columbian burial site that existed in El Caño, Panama, between AD 700 and AD 1000. We thought we had prepared well for the dig, but as you know …."

His voice trailed off as he finished the sentence. After taking a large swig of his bourbon, Sloane rubbed his eyebrows and the top of his cheekbones. Alec noticed he seemed blocked up and asked whether he had allergies.

Sloane shrugged. "I'm not sure. The doctor says it's recurrent, acute sinusitis. It's a real pain in the ass and the nasal spray I take doesn't last a full ten hours."

In response, Sloane removed a bottle of nasal spray from his pants pocket and blasted two squirts into each nostril. Paige looked away for a moment and then back after he sighed, "That's a bit better."

Sloane left minutes later to speak to Annette. His chair didn't stay empty for long. Marshall Weissman stopped by to chat and complained, "Sloane doesn't approve of my field of garbology either."

The DunBartons asked about his area of expertise and learned that garbologists examined modern landfills to figure out what refuse says about our society. Excitedly, Weissman explained, "At a dig in Tucson, my team discovered that 10% to 15% of garbage is food waste and that middle-income households disposed of the most. Middle class folks also spent less money on liquor compared to rich and poor families."

Alec found it fascinating and wondered how many showers Marshall had to take after spending a day at a public landfill. Alec and Paige had to excuse themselves shortly later. On the way out of the Constellation Lounge, Alec noticed the captain with Emily Irving at a secluded table. From the way they were looking at each other, Alec guessed that their student-teacher relationship had morphed into something more intimate.

While getting ready for bed, Alec and Paige talked about their evening. Now eager to attend the FAO's first lecture the following day, Alec remarked, "I don't think archaeologists are as dull as I had previously thought. All of them are quite different. What did you make of Aaron Sloane and Emily Irving?"

Paige was removing her eye makeup when she replied, "I don't care for Sloane. He's arrogant and doesn't like women. I could tell by the way he generally demeans the female members in his group and Annette Perkins in particular. I can't imagine what he was like with his wife! It might be the reason she sought comfort from others."

Alec kissed the top of Paige's head and caught sight of their reflection in her mirror. Sweetly, he asked, "I'll never cause you to stray."

Paige smiled, "Not if you know what's good for you. I expect you to always pamper me'"

Alec laughed and promised, "Come to bed, Lass. You're in for a pleasurable night."

At 9:30 AM, Alec made his way to his office. Though an hour late for work, Alec felt at peace with the world. He had slept well, enjoyed a leisurely breakfast with Paige, and was confident that the FAO members were *not* going to be a problem.

Boy, was he wrong!

Upon entering his office, Alec was met by the Chief of Security, Harold Zuma. The South African officer was tall, black, and in his mid-fifties. Zuma had transferred to the Pegasus about a year earlier.

The officer's expression was bleak as he uttered, "A passenger died last night. Dr. Abbot thinks he may have overdosed. Please follow me to the fellow's cabin."

Alec and the security chief took the elevator up to the Riviera Deck and walked down the corridor to Cabin 8028. The door was closed. On entering the room, Alec and Zuma had to step around a stretcher that was partially in the way.

The doctor was bent over the bed and looked up at the two men as they drew closer. At that moment, Alec could see the deceased patient was Aaron Sloane. Not terribly surprised it was Sloane, Alec launched into several questions. Answering one, Douglas announced, "It looks like a drug overdose. I'll have to run some tests to be certain."

Alec peered at the archaeologist's face. His glassy blue eyes were staring up at the ceiling. There was vomit on his pillow and the cabin's phone was dangling off its hook.

Despite the seriousness of the situation, Alec sang out,

No one knows what it's like
To be the bad man
To be the sad man
Behind blue eyes

No one knows what it's like
To be hated
To be fated
To telling only lies

But my dreams
They aren't as empty
As my conscience seems to be

I have hours, only lonely
My love is vengeance
That's never free

No one knows what it's like
To feel these feelings
Like I do
And I blame you

No one bites back as hard
On their anger
None of my pain and woe
Can show through

But my dreams
They aren't as empty
As my conscience seems to be

I have hours, only lonely
My love is vengeance
That's never free

When my fist clenches, crack it open
Before I use it and lose my cool
When I smile, tell me some bad news
Before I laugh and act like a fool

And if I swallow anything evil
Put your finger down my throat

And if I shiver, please give me a blanket
Keep me warm, let me wear your coat

No one knows what it's like
To be the bad man
To be the sad man
Behind blue eyes

In exasperation, Douglas cried out, "Now? You're doing this now?"

Sheepishly, Alec apologized and began to take pictures of the corpse and the surrounding area with his cell phone camera, He then donned a pair of medical gloves and helped the doctor and Zuma transfer the deceased to the rolling stretcher.

Sloane's body was as stiff as a board and his skin was the temperature of the air-conditioned suite. While they were heading to the crew elevator, Alec let them know, "I'm going to return to his cabin to take photographs of the entire room. I'll join you afterward."

The suite was relatively tidy. Over a chair was the pair of pants and shirt that Sloane had worn the evening before, Everything else was neatly put away in the drawers and closet. Sloane's toiletries were stacked on the bathroom shelves. There was one partially damp towel hanging on the back of the door and discarded items in the bathroom trashcan.

Upon going through it, Alec discovered crumpled tissues, dirty cotton swabs, and an empty bottle of Afrin nasal spray. If Sloane had overdosed, where was his drug paraphernalia? There were no pills, prescriptions, or otherwise, in the bathroom.

Beside the bed, Alec gently touched the end table wondering whether Sloane used cocaine. There was nothing, not even dust. The only thing, an arm's length away, was the cabin phone base and a second bottle of nasal spray.

Alec expected that Sloane's death was peaceful. Other than seeing a small amount of vomit on the pillow and the phone receiver hanging off the end table, the bed sheets were pretty tight and still tucked between the mattress and springs.

Still wearing medical gloves, Alec took the full bottle of Afrin nasal spray from the bedstand along with the empty one from the bathroom trash can. After closing the door, he made certain it locked behind him.

When Alec arrived at sickbay, he was directed to the ship's morgue by the nurse on duty. Alec could hear voices as he approached the room. Because Flagship Cruise Line catered to elderly clientele, who sometimes came aboard with heart disease and other infirmities, the Pegasus had cold storage for four deceased persons.

The morgue not only contained storage for the bodies but also a stainless-steel work table. Above the table were various instruments and medical devices. The doctor was taking the corpse's body temperature when Alec joined him and Officer Zuma.

On seeing Alec, Douglas stated, "I think he's been dead ten to twelve hours; His muscles were completely stiff, and his body has cooled to 83°F."

Harold added, "I've spoken to my team. According to Sloane's keycard, he entered his room at 10:45 PM and no one entered until the cabin steward checked on him with Annette Perkins this morning. The woman couldn't reach him on his cabin phone and asked his steward to make sure he was alright when he didn't show up for breakfast in the dining room at eight."

Alec nodded and asked Dr. Abbot, "What makes you think he overdosed? I couldn't find any signs he took drugs. And, he *wasn't* the suicidal type. If anything, he was the sort of man to take someone else's life."

In response, the doctor went into a long-winded explanation stating, "Sloane's pupils were the size of pinpricks and there was frothy fluid around his nose and mouth, His diaphragm, chest wall, and upper airway were more rigid than they should have been for the time he was in rigor. I believe Sloane experienced wooden chest syndrome prior to dying. A fentanyl overdose often causes it."

Frustrated, Alec set down both bottles of nasal spray on the steel table and asked, "Could these be responsible? The full one was on his bedside table and the empty one in the bathroom trash can."

Douglas held the full bottle of Afin up to the light and replied, "It's easy to test. I have fentanyl strips."

Alec watched the doctor place a test strip on the table and made a move to sniff the contents of the bottle.

Dr. Abbot slapped his hand away and scolded, "If it is fentanyl, the fumes can give you an opioid high. The drug comes in many forms—pills, liquid, patches, lozenges, drops, and nasal spray. Many cancer sufferers regard it as a godsend. It's a shame, nowadays, that people get these illicit narcotics on the street. So many have died needlessly!"

The doctor then placed two droplets of the sinus liquid on the test strip and waited a few minutes for the result. Not long after, one single red line appeared, and Douglas confirmed, "It's fentanyl. I can't tell whether it's prescription grade or not, but I'm very sure this substance caused his death."

Alec shook his head and explained, "I saw Sloane spray both nostrils twice last night. He had no reaction to it and complained that the medicine didn't last a full ten hours."

Douglas then conducted another test on the nearly empty bottle. There was enough fluid to test the substance and the doctor pronounced, "This nasal spray has no fentanyl in it. Sloane must have used the medicine in this bottle when you witnessed him take it."

It became obvious to both men that sometime between 11:00 PM and 1:00 AM, Aaron Sloane disposed of his empty and ineffective nasal spray in his cabin and opened a new one that contained enough fentanyl to kill him.

CHAPTER FOUR

▼

"Another One Bites the Dust"
Words & Music by John Deacon
Genre: Funk Rock, Released: August 1980

Tuesday Morning—6th of February
Over the next two hours, Alec had to accomplish several tasks. His first order of business was to speak to Sloane's cabin steward. The fellow was unable to give Alec much information about his charge's overnight activities since he went off duty at 9:00 PM the previous evening.

When the steward arrived on duty, the Do Not Disturb sign was on Sloane's doorknob. In broken English, the young man explained, "Mr. Sloane, not too friendly. He say little since he board."

Alec thanked him and asked, "When did Ms. Perkins approach you to check on him?"

The fellow responded, "It was few minutes past nine. I was in the hall and cleaning two rooms over. She was mad that he missed their breakfast. The sign was on the door. After I knocked and no one answered, I used my keycard. He did not move. I told her he might be sick, and I contacted security and the doctor."

Nodding, Alec inquired, "What was her reaction to your words."

Having more problem expressing himself, the steward said, "She not happy and left in bad temper. Did I do something wrong?"

Alec assured him that he had handled the situation perfectly and warned, "The cabin must remain locked for the duration of the cruise. The police will want to examine it on the ship's return to Florida on February 15th. Leave it as it is and don't let anyone go in."

The steward shook his head and promised, "I'll make sure."

From the cabin, Alec headed to the Hudson Room where the FAO were holding their morning meeting. Since it had just turned eleven, only Perkins and a few remaining archaeologists were still in attendance.

Alec drew Annette away from the others and said, "I'm afraid Aaron Sloane died last night."

Annette merely frowned and replied, "I suspected he was sick or worse when I didn't see him at breakfast or this meeting. Do you know what happened?"

Though Alec was certain that Sloane had overdosed on fentanyl, he withheld the information and answered, "I'll give your group an update at 3:00 o'clock after your archeology lecture in the Starlight Lounge. Did anyone at your morning meeting ask about Sloane's whereabouts?"

Annette scoffed, "Victor Bristow. The others seemed relieved. At our gathering, we reviewed what we planned to say and do at this afternoon's event. Since Sloane wasn't going to be part of the presentation, no one missed him. I told the group he was probably sick."

"Very good," Alec injected and then asked, "Do you have an emergency contact for Aaron Sloane?"

Perkins handed Alec a slip of paper saying, "I had a feeling you might need this." On it was the name Franklin Sloane, along with the man's phone number, email, and physical address.

As Alec walked away, four questions came to his mind. Why did Perkins have Sloane's emergency contact information on her person? Did she know he was dead when she left his cabin? Why was Victor Bristow the only one to ask about Sloane? And, finally, did Victor poison Sloane and want confirmation he was dead?

At five minutes to one, Alec knocked on the captain's meeting room door. Security Officer Zuma was already present and let him in. Stewart, seated at an oval table, pronounced, "We'll begin once Dr. Abbot gets here. This is all new to me. In all my years of service with FCL, I have never had an incident like this happen before!"

Alec apologized, "I'm sorry, Captain Stewart."

His response seemed to anger Stewart and, raising his voice, the captain spouted, "I was told about you. You're a bad penny! Everywhere you go, there's a murder!"

The captain's tirade came to an end when Dr. Abbot arrived. While the three men joined the captain at the table, Stewart gained control over his emotions and questioned the doctor, "Can you tell me anything more about the man's death?"

Douglas began. "Alec found two bottles of Afrin nasal spray in Sloane's cabin. The medicine is commonly used for sinus congestion. The nearly empty spray bottle contained *no* fentanyl. The full one did.

"I can't be absolutely sure that Aaron Sloane was murdered. He definitely died from a fentanyl overdose. It's possible he placed the drug in the nasal spray himself and used too much. If he was an addict, I saw no signs of it on his body. Before preparing his corpse for the freezer. I examined it pretty closely.

"There were no needle marks on Sloane's skin and his nasal passages were relatively clear. Fentanyl nasal sprays are used by patients that have breakthrough cancer pain and can't take other meds. Lazanda makes a pharmaceutical fentanyl nasal spray, but the recommended dose is a single spray in one nostril. It's not for people who have breathing problems or to be used more than four times in twenty-four hours."

Since no one interrupted him, Douglas continued, "It's a shame we didn't get to Sloane when he first overdosed. I have Narcan in the infirmary. It could have saved him if administered early enough. Since his phone was off the hook, I can only surmise that he tried to call for help and passed out before he could contact the infirmary."

"I see," the captain responded icily and asked Alec. "Did you find any illicit drugs in Sloane's cabin?"

Succinctly, Alec replied, "I conducted a preliminary search this morning and will go back to his quarters this afternoon to test all of Sloane's toiletries with the doctor's fentanyl strips. On my previous search, I was unable to find an empty Afrin box or its plastic safety seal. It leads me to believe that the full bottle did not come directly from a pharmacy. The wrapping must have been disposed of at another time or by someone who gave Sloane the tainted bottle."

Upon being asked how he planned to proceed, Alec outlined, "I'm going to investigate Sloane's death under the assumption that he was murdered and consider his fellow archaeologists suspects or witnesses. At two o'clock, I'm going to attend the FAO panel discussion in the Starlight Lounge. I've told Annette Perkins that I will speak to the group afterward and let them know what befell Mr. Sloane."

Alec continued, "I will, of course, contact the Fort Lauderdale's Homicide Department and liaise with Dan McGill, a fellow I've worked with before. He'll want to alert the decedent's next of kin and for me to give him a list of Sloane's close acquaintances on this cruise."

Captain Stewart demanded, "I'll want thorough progress reports!"

With that said, he excused Alec and Dr. Abbot to speak to Officer Zuma alone.

When the office door closed behind him, Douglas quipped, "That's another one you can add to your list of murders."

Skipping the first verse, Alec belted out,

Another one bites the dust
Another one bites the dust
And another one gone, and another one gone
Another one bites the dust, yeah
Hey, I'm gonna get you, too
Another one bites the dust

How do you think I'm gonna get along
Without you when you're gone?
You took me for everything that I had
And kicked me out on my own

Are you happy, are you satisfied?
How long can you stand the heat?
Out of the doorway the bullets rip
To the sound of the beat

Look out!

Another one bites the dust
Another one bites the dust
And another one gone, and another one gone
Another one bites the dust
Hey, I'm gonna get you, too
Another one bites the dust

Hey!
Oh, take it
Bite the dust
Bite the dust, yeah

Another one bites the dust
Another one bites the dust, ow
Another one bites the dust, hey hey
Another one bites the dust, hey-eh-eh

Shout!

There are plenty of ways that you can hurt a man
And bring him to the ground
You can beat him, you can cheat him
You can treat him bad and leave him when he's down, yeah

But I'm ready, yes, I'm ready for you
I'm standing on my own two feet
Out of the doorway the bullets rip
Repeating to the sound of the beat

Oh, yeah

Another one bites the dust
Another one bites the dust
And another one gone, and another one gone
Another one bites the dust, yeah
Hey, I'm gonna get you, too
Another one bites the dust

Douglas merely ignored him and said, "I haven't had anything to eat since this morning. Do you want to join me for lunch?"

Alec glanced at his wristwatch and noted it was 1:25 PM. He agreed, "I have about twenty minutes to grab a sandwich from the Lido Deck." Together, two men took the stairs one flight up to the buffet.

The Starlight Lounge was occupied by a small number of passengers. It was a sea day and an hour earlier, the ship had presented a movie on the building of the Panama Canal in 1914 and its later expansion in 2016.

Alec guessed that the few remaining people in the audience were interested in archaeology, too. Also eager to learn, Alec took a seat in the middle of the auditorium.

On the left side of the stage were four members of the FAO. They included Annette Perkins, Marshall Weissman, Victor Bristow, and his daughter Jennifer. To their right was a large film screen with the group's name emblazed on it.

With a microphone in her hand, Faith, the cruise director, walked out from the wings and welcomed the attendees to the first of three lectures on the topic of archaeology. After introducing the FAO panelists, Faith let Annette take over. Looking professional,

Perkins announced, "Today, we're going to introduce you to the basics.

"Archaeologists learn about past human behavior by studying material evidence that was left behind. The material evidence, we call artifacts, include possessions, residues, and anything visible or tangible. It can be a seed or a pyramid, kitchen garbage or gold craftwork, or the hair from a mummified corpse. Paleontologists are different from us. They study dinosaur bones and other fossils left before humans inhabited the earth."

Annette went on to say, "Some archaeologists concentrate on a particular place like Egypt or Mesoamerica, others on sites such as caves and pyramids, and still others on a specific time period. Prehistoric archaeology covers the time period before written records were created.

"Historic archaeologists specialize in literate cultures, which include early Chinese, Greek, and Roman civilizations that developed over the last five thousand years. Not all early societies were the same. Some developed writing before others."

Annette then had Jennifer begin a slide presentation showing the massive amounts of supplies and equipment that was needed to conduct an archaeological survey. It included shovels, flagging tape, machetes, maps, waterproof markers, measuring devices, first-aid kits, water, food, and a reliable vehicle. After seeing it and several dig sites, Alec realized that archaeologists needed to be adventurous and not too concerned with their own creature comforts.

Marshall spoke next and told the group, "I'm the resident nerd." Despite his goofy appearance and overly enthusiastic tone, he seemed to entrance the audience members. Over a fifteen-minute period, he talked about various dating methods and explained that radiocarbon dating only worked on artifacts containing carbon and were less than 50,000 years old. Stone, metal, and pottery had to be dated by other means through direct, indirect, absolute, historic, and relative methods. He went on to clarify what each term meant.

Alec was surprised to hear that potassium argon dating was available to measure the age of items over a billion years old. Since bones contain potassium, skeletons over 50,000 years old could be dated. Those bones were able to tell archaeologists the sex and age of people, their height, health, cultural practices, hygiene, diseases, and DNA, if a large enough sample was present.

Dried feces, known as coprolites, was instrumental in letting archaeologists know what people ingested. From a sample, they could determine a person's general health, where they got their food, whether they produced or gathered it, what intestinal parasites they carried, and the kinds of pollen in the area.

To drive home the point, Marshall explained, "Tuberculosis was once thought to be a disease that Europeans brought to the Americas in the sixteenth century. From DNA, gathered from bone lesions and dry lung tissue, we now know that the tuberculosis germ was present in the New World *before* the Europeans arrived."

When Victor Bristow rose to speak, Alec was momentarily disappointed. It turned out that he was equally interesting in another way. He handed out a timeline covering the existence of humankind from their earliest beginnings to the recent past.

As he spoke, Jennifer conducted a power point presentation of artifacts from different periods and places. The timeline read:

Dates	Culture	Artifacts	Africa	West Asia (Middle East)	East Asia	Europe	North America	South America
Over 500,000 Million BC	Earliest Hominids (East Africa), Scavenging, forging, possible hunting	Pebble tools, handaxes, other stone tools, animal bones, bones of hominids, footprints, preserved cave sites	Olorgesailie, (Kenya)		Zhoukoudian, (China)			
500,000 BC to 250,000 BC	Neanderthals, etc. Hunting, gathering, and small social groups	Spear points, other stone, bone, and wooden artifacts. Caves and other small sites	Many Sites	Shanidar Cave (Iraq)	Niah Cave (Borneo)	Atapuerca, Torralba, (Spain), Terra Amata, (France)		

The Singing Sleuth Digs Up the Past

Dates	Culture	Artifacts	Africa	West Asia (Middle East)	East Asia	Europe	North America	South America
250,000 BC to 35,000 BC	Homo Sapiens to present day Hunting Ice Age game, gathering, fishing, small social groups	Fine points, other tools of stone, bone, wood, antler, ivory figurines, cave art, and small sites	Many Sites	Many Sites	Many Sites	Lascaux Cave (France) and many sites	Clovis (New Mexico) and many other Paleo-Indian sites	Monte Verde (Chile) and many other Paleo-Indian sites
35,000 BC to 8,000 BC	Hunting modern animals, gathering plants, fishing, shellfishing, larger social groups	Stone tools, pottery, utilitarian & decorative artifacts, small campsites and structures, some large settlements and rare earth works	Many Sites	Many Sites	Jomon Culture (Japan)	Vedbaek (Denmark)		
8,000 BC to 7,000 BC	Earliest food production in Old World, large villages	Remains of earliest domesticated plants and animals, farming and herding tools, houses, village sites	Sites along the Nile River, (Egypt)	Catalhoyuk, (Turkey), Abu Hureyra, (Syria), Jericho, (Israel)	Mehrgarh, (Pakistan), sites on Yellow and Yangtze Rivers (China)	Many Sites	Windover, (Florida), Watson Brake, (Louisiana), shell midden sites	Coastal shell midden sites, large villages
7,000 BC to 5,500 BC	Copper and Bronze Age in Old World, large villages, towns	Metal artifacts common, a few signs of warfare	Many Sites			Varna, (Bulgaria), Otzi, the Ice Man, (Italy)		
5,500 BC to 3,500 BC	True civilizations in the Old World	Cities, great monuments, sculpures, writing systems seen on artifacts, finds showing trade over long distances	Egyptian kingdom, pryamids	Uruk, Ur, other Mesopotamia states	Indis Valley civilization, (Pakistan & India), An-yang, (China)	Stonehenge, (England), Malta megalithic monuments	Poverty Point (Louisania), Early farming settlements (Mexico and Central America)	Aspero and Caral (Peru), and other farming sites with pyramids
3,500 BC to 1,500 BC	True civilizations in the New World, continuing in Old World		Egypt, Nubia regional kingdoms			Bronze Age Greek Civilization	Ancestral Pueblo farming (Southwest U.S.), Mound building East Olmec civilization (Mexico)	Chavin civilization (Peru)
1,500 BC to AD 100	Later civilizations (some cultures continued a simpler foraging life)	Historic and prehistoric settlements, material remains of everyday life not recorded in history		Succeeding states	Qin empire, succeeding dynastic empires	Roman Empire	Hopewell & other mound builders (Eastern U.S.), Maya, Teotihuacan, other city-states in Mesoamerica	Moche, Nazca states, then Tiwanaku and Wari empires, (Peru and Bolivia)
AD 100 to AD 1,000			Great Zimbabwe		Angkor states, (Cambodia), and other historic archaeology	Medieval and more recent historic archaeology	Cahokia (Illinois), Moundville, (Alabama), Chaco and Mesa Verde (Southwest U.S.), late Mesoamerican civilizations like Aztec in Mexico	Chimu state, Inca empire, (Peru)

The lecture ended soon after. Annette reminded the passengers that there was going to be an Archaeology Quiz containing the material they had just covered the following day at the Explorer's Club. She also invited them to return for their second lecture on Friday, February 9th.

As the passengers were filing out, Alec rushed to the front of the lounge and requested, "Can all the FAO members remain here a moment? The archaeologists in the audience must have been aware of the upcoming meeting and moved to the front of the auditorium.

When everyone was seated, Alec stated, "My name is Alec DunBarton. I'm the controller on the Pegasus and a liaison officer between Flagship Cruise Line and the police department in Fort Lauderdale." With that said, he added, "I have the sad duty to tell you that Mr. Aaron Sloane was pronounced dead this morning."

Alec waited while the surprised responses died down and then continued, "The doctor believes that Mr. Sloane overdosed on fentanyl. At this time, we don't know whether it was an accident, suicide, or something more sinister."

Again, Alec stopped, this time to take questions. Several of Sloane's fellow members seemed impervious to the news, others reacted emotionally, and a few expressed disbelief.

Alec centered his attention on the few archaeologists who had bumped heads with Sloane over the last two days. He was cognizant, too, that Sloane could have been killed by a passenger who had no affiliation with the FAO or a person who wasn't on the cruise. The victim's nasal spray could have been tampered with prior to the sailing.

After taking questions and stretching the truth when it suited him, Alec concluded, "I'll be joining your group activities to gather information that will help me and the police determine whether Mr. Sloane's death was intentional or unintentional. If any of you would like to speak to me privately, my office is on the Lower Promenade Deck."

While the FAO members departed, Annette approached Alec and whispered, "I think that went pretty well. Is there anything I can do?"

Now seeing the intrepid president as an ally, Alec smiled and asked, "Can you give me a complete list of your members and check off those on this cruise? Also, let me know which ones might have had reason to dislike Aaron Sloane."

Perkins winked in response. "That will be a long list! I'll email it to you."

CHAPTER FIVE

▼

"Kokomo"
Words & Music by John Phillips,
Terry Melcher, Mike Love and Scott McKenzie
Genre: Soft Rock, Released: June 1988

Tuesday Evening—6th of February

Alec was on the computer in his office when he received the FAO membership list from Annette Perkins. Besides the twenty-two names of those sailing on the Pegasus, she included an additional sixty people who were past and current members. She also delineated those who were more intimately involved with Sloane. Alec was not surprised that he was already aware of them.

Armed with the list, Alec composed an email to Dan McGill at the Fort Lauderdale Homicide Department. Before sending it off, he inserted Annette's file, the name and address of Sloane's brother, and photographs of the "crime" scene.

The message read:

Subj: Another Murder on the Pegasus?
Date: 6th of February, 6:18:51 PM AST
From: AlecDunBarton@aol.com
To: Dan.McGill@coflso.net

Dan,

I'm going to need your help again. This morning, we discovered the body of Aaron Sloane, a member of FAO (the Florida Archaeology Organization). Twenty-one of his fellow FAO members are currently sailing with us. The doctor believes Sloane died between 11:00 PM and 1:00 AM since he was in full rigor when we discovered him this morning.

I found a non-prescription bottle of Afrin nasal spray beside his bed and an empty one in his trash can. The doctor tested both and only the spray bottle on his bedstand contained fentanyl citrate. Dr. Abbot will send you both nasal sprays and a sample of Sloane's blood from Aruba tomorrow.

This afternoon, I returned to his sealed cabin to test all of Sloane's toiletries with fentanyl test strips. I was unable to find any suspicious drugs. Aaron Sloane was not well liked by his fellow associates. He was pompous and demeaned others with looks and words. I've inserted a complete list of people (past and present) who were/are members of FAO.

I'm particularly concerned about six members who had a close acquaintance with Sloane. They are Victor Bristow, Jennifer Bristow (Victor's daughter), Michael Donovan, Marshall Weissman, Emily Irving, and Annette Perkins (president of the FAO). Let me know if any of them have a criminal record and were prescribed fentanyl. Because the illegal drug is so abundant, I wonder if we'll ever learn where it came from.

My new captain, Charles Stewart, asked me to monitor the group's activities at the beginning of the cruise (before Sloane died). The captain is an amateur archaeologist and has worked on a few digs with Emily Irving. Their relationship may be closer than that of teacher and student. I'll try to find out whether Irving had a more personal reason to dislike Sloane.

Dr. Abbot will email you the package's tracking number. It's possible the fentanyl in the nose spray was not potent enough to kill him. Hopefully, we'll know more when you receive the toxicology report on his blood. Though Sloane could have accidently overdosed, he wasn't the kind of man to take drugs. He was even less likely to commit suicide.

Thank you in advance. I know I've been a pain in the butt.

Regards,
Alec

After rereading the email, Alec sent it off and checked the time. It was approaching six-thirty and he was hungry. Paige had dined earlier as she was among the officers that Captain Stewart was going to introduce at his Gala Welcome Party in the Starlight Lounge at seven.

Again, Alec had to grab a quick meal and was glad to find a short line at the ship's pizzeria. He downed a glass of iced tea and personal-sized pepperoni pizza in twenty minutes and quickly made his way to the large auditorium.

Along the way, Alec passed passengers in festive outfits waiting to be photographed in front of scenic backdrops. On the first sea day, FCL passengers were given an opportunity to enjoy complimentary champagne, red wine, or fruit punch at the captain's party. Though the appetizers had grown smaller and the drinks less potent over the years, the affair always proved to be popular.

Alec arrived a few minutes late and watched the presentation from the back of the lounge. The auditorium was very crowded. Stewart was on the stage and had just introduced Dr. Douglas Abbot, dressed in his formal uniform. Paige followed in one of her more dazzling evening gowns.

She took Alec's breath away. They had been married for two and a half years, and Alec considered themselves honeymooners. There was never a time that Alec wasn't thankful for her. Paige had been by his side while he mourned the death of his first wife and daughter who were killed by a drunk driver in London. She had helped him pick up the pieces of his shattered life and made it easier for him to recreate himself.

Alec managed to get a glass of champagne from a passing server and waited for the ceremony to end. At its close, Paige waved to Alec from the front of the auditorium and caught up with him moments later. Though Alec wanted to give her a kiss, he restrained himself. The captain and his entourage were steps behind her.

Stewart eyed Alec as he approached him and said, "I trust you have everything in hand."

Alec nodded, "I've informed the FAO members of Sloane's death and emailed all relevant information to my police contact in Fort Lauderdale. Dr. Abbot is going to post a sample of Sloane's blood from Aruba tomorrow along with the two Afrin nasal spray bottles."

Looking less testy, Stewart sighed, "Keep me posted."

Paige waited for the captain to leave and then asked Alec, "Are you planning to pursue any of the archaeologists tomorrow? I'm off in the afternoon and the ship is going to dock in Oranjestad at 1:00 o'clock. Would you mind if I joined you? The last time we did any sleuthing together was six months ago."

Alec laughed and remarked, "I think I've created a monster."

Unable to catch up with Douglas in the Starlight Lounge, the DunBartons took the stairs to the infirmary. After reassuring the captain that he had everything under control, Alec wanted to make sure that the doctor had his package ready to be posted from Aruba.

Dr. Abbot, still in his dress uniform, was full of information and explained, "I spoke to a forensics technician in Florida today. He told me I can send a dried sample of Sloane's blood. It's certainly a lot easier than mailing it in liquid form. Wet blood samples must be tested within eight hours to be viable."

Upon hearing that, Alec said, "I'm glad you checked. Send the package overnight or as quick as you. Captain Stewart is on my back."

Douglas sympathized, "There's a FedEx International office about four miles from the cruise terminal. It's on Sabana Blanco 70 A. I'll get it there by 2:00 o'clock."

Changing the subject, he inquired, "What are your plans tonight? Do you want to join Regina and me for a drink?"

Paige gazed at Alec and asked whether he was up to it. She needed to change her shoes, which were pinching her toes, and Alec admitted to feeling "wiped out" after a full day of running around. Alec turned down his offer and said, "We want to book a shore excursion for tomorrow and get to bed early."

From the infirmary, the pair headed to the Shore Excursion Desk and learned it was closed till the morning. Unwilling to wait, Alec and Paige returned to their cabin to see what tours were being offered on the ship's intranet. Besides excursions, passengers could see the daily activities, special events, restaurant menus, their purchase history, and other valuable information.

After examining the open tours, Alec selected a five-hour excursion entitled, "Hidden Gems of Aruba." Luckily, it wasn't fully booked.

Seconds later, Paige disrobed and headed over to the bathroom to take her nightly bath. It gave Alec time to stretch out on the bed and read about all the places they were going to visit on the Dutch island.

Alec awoke to the sound of Paige telling him to remove his clothes and get under the covers. Once he was settled, he received a kiss for his efforts. Alec fell back to sleep in minutes.

At eight o'clock, the alarm awakened Alec. Paige was already stirring in their mini kitchen and called, "I'm brewing your coffee."

When she brought over his huge mug of black coffee, she added, "You slept like the dead!"

Alec adjusted his pillow to pull himself up to a sitting position. Before taking the cup, he remarked, "I feel energized this morning and ready to tackle the day."

Paige tidied up the room and remained just long enough to finish dressing. Before departing, she reminded Alec, "I have a seminar at 11:00 AM, and I'll meet you for lunch at the Lido Buffet at twelve thirty."

Alec nodded and realized that he couldn't dally either. After finishing his coffee with some day-old croissants that Paige had squirreled away, he got ready for the day. His first stop was his office to check on Regina.

She was hard at work sending reports to corporate headquarters in Southampton, England. She raised her head when Alec entered the room and teased, "Last night, Douglas told me about your latest murder. As usual, I'm expected to do your work as well as mine?"

Although Alec felt a bit sorry for his assistant, he didn't try to hide his enthusiasm and stated, "It's been six months since I've had to solve a suspicious death. I hope I haven't lost my touch."

Regina beamed, "Not you! I have full confidence that you'll be able to name the killer by the time the ship docks in Florida."

For the next hour, Alec showed Regina how far he had gotten on his own work. When the stacks of paper were transferred from his desk to hers, he excused himself.

While Alec walked to the door, she asked, "So, where are you going?"

With a smile, he answered, "I'm going to test my archaeology knowledge. The FAO is having a trivia contest at the Explorer's Club at ten o'clock."

Sarcastically, Regina rejoined, "That's so nice for you."

The Explorer's Club was about halfway filled when Alec entered the lounge. Before taking a seat, he stopped to pick up a trivia form and pencil from the bar. Faith Rossi was standing beside it with Annette Perkins and Emily Irving. Several of the FAO members were in the audience and seated together.

At eleven, Faith addressed the group, "I'm glad you have joined us for our first archaeological trivia contest. Unlike our usual games, I'll be asking twenty *multiple choice* questions. Instead of being in groups of six, we want you to test your individual knowledge.

"For some questions, I'm going to direct you to the film screen to my left. Faith stopped to point it out and resumed, "On it, we'll be projecting photos of a few notable artifacts. From the Florida Archaeology Organization, the winner will receive a free tour for two in Curaçao, valued at two hundred dollars."

There were cheers from the crowd as most prizes given at trivia contests were not worth much and included items like keychains, luggage tags, magnets, and lanyards. Faith continued, "With me are the president and the treasurer of the FAO. As usual, my answer is the final answer."

Alec found the game pretty difficult despite the four multiple-choice answers. The questions covered material given the previous day. Alec laughed when Faith asked the definition of a coprolite. The harder questions revolved around the timeline that Victor had handed out covering the period from 500,000 BC to the present.

At the completion of the game, the passengers were asked to exchange papers with another guest and to award five points for each correct answer. While Faith gave the answers, there were oohs and aahs.

When the quiz papers were returned, Faith asked, "Has anyone attained a score of sixty?" Many hands, including Alec's went up. She continued until only one person remained with a score of ninety-five. It was Captain Stewart.

From his seat, he greeted the group and announced, "The award will go to the couple who got ninety. As an amateur archaeologist, I'm glad to see passengers interested in the subject. I hope you will continue to enjoy the archaeology lectures on this Panama Canal cruise."

There were applause while an elderly couple picked up their shore excursion vouchers. Alec watched the captain as he helped Emily Irving pack up the projection slides.

Although Alec had hoped to slip out of the room, Stewart summoned him before he could make a getaway. He wanted to know what Alec got on the quiz. After learning that Alec had scored an eighty-five and planned to take the "Hidden Gems of Aruba" excursion at two thirty, the captain remarked, "Satisfactory."

Alec departed, uncertain whether Stewart was happier with his score or tour choice.

Alec met Paige as planned for lunch on the Lido Deck. The pair chose a filling meal of penne a la vodka, garlic bread, and a side salad. Certain they would not need a snack on the bus, Alec and Paige returned to their cabin to change into their civies and pack up Paige's tote bag.

Paige's canvas bag was bulging with their sun hats, sunscreen, camera phones, and water bottles when Alec lifted it up and beckoned Paige, "Let's go, Lass. We're supposed to meet the tour group at 2:15 PM outside the cruise ship terminal."

Upon closing the door behind them, Alec sang out,

Aruba, Jamaica, ooh I wanna take ya
Bermuda, Bahama, come on pretty mama
Key Largo, Montego,
baby why don't we go,
Jamaica

Off the Florida Keys
There's a place called Kokomo
That's where you wanna go
to get away from it all
Bodies in the sand,
tropical drink melting in your hand
We'll be falling in love
to the rhythm of a steel drum band
Down in Kokomo

Aruba, Jamaica, ooh I wanna take you to
Bermuda, Bahama, come on pretty mama
Key Largo Montego,
baby why don't we go
Ooh I wanna take you down to Kokomo,
We'll get there fast
and then we'll take it slow
That's where we wanna go,
way down in Kokomo.

Martinique, that Monserrat mystique...

We'll put out to sea
and we'll perfect our chemistry
By and by we'll defy
a little bit of gravity
Afternoon delight,

cocktails and moonlit nights
That dreamy look in your eye,
give me a tropical contact high
Way down in Kokomo

When he finished the song, Paige remarked, "You make catching a killer sound very romantic."

Alec smiled, "There's no reason it can't be both."

CHAPTER SIX

▼

"The Caves of Altamira"
Words & Music by Donald Fagan and Walter Becker
Genre: Progressive Rock, Released: January 1976

Wednesday Afternoon—7th of February

The DunBartons stepped off the ship after flashing their key cards at the security kiosk. It was a lovely day with the temperatures in the low eighties. The port shops and the Aruba Welcome Desk were steps away from the gangway. The building had some American fast-food restaurants, a coffee bar, and countless stores selling souvenir straw hats, aloe, and colorful clothing.

Buses were lined up outside the building. Alec and Paige followed the handheld signs for the "Hidden Gems of Aruba" excursion. Paige, hurrying behind Alec's fast strides, protested, "This is getting less romantic by the minute. Why are you rushing?"

Alec slowed down and apologized, "The Bristows are ahead of us and in line for our bus. I'd like to get a seat near them and eavesdrop if we can."

Though six passengers separated Alec from his quarry, he and Paige were able to take seats to their right on the same row. While sitting in the aisle, Alec turned to Victor Bristow and said, "I see we're on the same tour. Is this your first time in Aruba?"

Victor, with his deadpan expression, replied, "I've been here several times with my wife. This is a first for Jennifer."

At the mention of her name, Jennifer gave Alec a smile that showed off her attractive dimples. Alec couldn't help wondering how such a somber father could have produced such a charming child.

Alec refrained from conversing while other passengers walked down the aisle to seek seats at the rear of the coach. Before Alec could say anything more, the tour guide came aboard and started to count the number of his charges. He then spoke to a person waiting outside and invited, "We have room for one more."

Alec was pleased to see the straggler was Michael Donovan.

As Donovan passed Bristow's row, he gave Jennifer a huge smile before finding the last seat on the bus.

Addressing his passengers, the tour guide said in a pleasant singsong voice, "Welcome to Aruba, One Happy Island. My name is Benjamin, and I will be taking you to Arikok National Park, southeast of us, the Lourdes Grotto, and finally, the California Lighthouse on the other side of my island."

Benjamin further explained, "I was born on the island and moved to Holland when I was in my twenties. I returned years later to run a cab company. Until 1986, Aruba belonged to the Kingdom of the Netherlands. Now it's a separate country but not a sovereign state. It means we have our own government but also must follow the Kingdom's laws regarding foreign affairs and defense."

On the twenty-minute ride, passengers also learned that the language of the ABC islands—Aruba, Bonaire, and Curaçao spoke Papiamento and Dutch. Papiamento, a creole language, was composed of Spanish, Portuguese, English, Arawak Indian, and African words.

Benjamin gave a brief history of the island, too. Though the Spanish discovered it in 1499, colonizers realized that the island wasn't a good place to establish plantations. The land was barren with no natural irrigation. The annual rainfall was less than seventeen inches per year. The Spanish declared Aruba, Bonaire, and Curaçao, *islas inútiles*, meaning useless islands, due to their lack of mineral wealth.

Because Aruba was seventeen miles from the coast of Venezuela and the country had supplied the Dutch with needed salt, the Netherlands took control of the land in 1636. The Dutch recruited the Caquetio Indians from Northwestern Venezuela to build farms and raise cattle for meat, which could be sold and shipped to other islands.

The landscape became a lot drier when the bus entered Arikok National Park. There was an abundance of thorny, long, poll-like cacti that tilted at odd angles. Benjamin rose to explain, "We're on our way to the first stop, Guadirikiri Cave.

"Once you ascend the rough stone steps to the cave, we'll have about twenty minutes to explore the two large chambers. If you use your camera flashlight, keep it directed to the floor. We don't want to disturb the fruit bats."

Many of the passengers thought he was kidding and learned to their disdain that the cave was full of bats that consumed mosquitos and crawling insects that lived in dark, moist recesses.

Paige's noise wrinkled in disgust while Alec laughed. She looked even more horrified when the bus stopped in front of the cave. Some of the stone steps leading up to the entrance were about fifteen inches high, roughly hewn, and missing handrails in several places.

On seeing a woman older than herself climb the steps, Paige agreed to follow Alec with the rest of the sightseers. After helping Paige find her footing in the first chamber, Alec became cognizant of the cool temperature and marveled at stalactites and stalagmites.

Paige voiced, "This place is rather romantic."

Overhearing her, the guide announced, "There's a myth that an Indian chief locked his daughter in Quadirikiri when she fell in love with an unacceptable suitor. Though they both died, it's said that their souls escaped through a hole in the chamber's dome."

When they followed him into the second section, he pointed to the ceiling, and added, "We're sure the couple made it to heaven."

Paige and Alec looked up and saw blue limestone in the shape of a heart, highlighted against a pinkish-brown wall.

Alec, who had momentarily lost track of the Bristows and Michael Donovan, noted that Victor was closely examining a stalagmite. Jennifer and Michael seemed to have other things on their minds and Alec guessed it wasn't speleology.

A short time later, Benjamin rounded up his group and watched them cautiously take the steps down to the bus. Once everyone was seated on the coach, a passenger asked, "Aren't caves supposed to be at ground level?"

Benjamin replied that the island was formed about 100 to 65 million years ago, during the Upper Cretaceous period. Aruba and its sister islands were under a volcanic ridge. When they emerged from the ocean, much of the land remained underwater or at sea level. The caves, once full of water, continued to rise.

Paige patted Alec's knee in response and said, "Now I understand why I had to climb *up* those awful steps."

While the bus continued to nearby Fontein Cave, Benjamin explained that the cave contained Pre-Columbian petroglyphs. The Arawak Indians painted birds and other creatures more than 1,000 years ago."

Laughing, he added, "You'll also see graffiti that dates from the early 1800s. This cave is more accessible than the last one through an opening in the cliff, and it's gates protect it from more modern vandals."

At this cave, a park guide took over from Benjamin and showed the group a nearby fresh water pond that was surrounded by greenery. The trees created shade and gave cover to goats and deer that came by to drink. Paige was surprised that the animals seemed undaunted by the number of humans watching them.

Enjoying the peaceful moment, Alec looked around once again and saw that Victor did not look happy. His daughter was with the underwater archaeologist. At the urging of the park guide, Donovan removed his sandals and let tiny fish in the natural pool give his feet a pedicure. Jennifer delighted in Michael's reaction and Victor looked even more peeved.

The group was then taken back to the Fontein Cave to explore its wonders. The Arawak natives, known as Caqueto, had decorated the rock faces and ceilings with brownish-red paint. It's believed that they used the cave to hide from enemies, perform tribal rituals, and hold assemblies.

Alec managed to walk beside Victor on the way out of the cave and asked if he had seen other cave art in Spain or France. The reserved fellow's eyes lit up as he responded, "I was allowed to visit the Cave of Altamira in the early 2000s. They had to close it to the public when the carbon dioxide and water vapor from the visitor's breath started to damage the artwork. It's a real shame."

Since the two men continued their conversation on the bus, Alec took Jennifer's seat and she ended up next to Paige. While listening to Victor explain how hunters and gatherers lived 35,000 years ago, the Steely Dan song came to Alec's mind.

Unable to keep the lyrics to himself, he sang,

I recall when I was small
How I spent my days alone
The busy world was not for me
So I went and found my own
I would climb the garden wall
With a candle in my hand
I'd hide inside a hall of rock and sand

On the stone an ancient hand
In a faded yellow green
Made alive a worldly wonder
Often told but never seen
Now and ever bound to labor
On the sea and in the sky
Every man and beast appeared
A friend as real as I

Before the fall when they wrote it on the wall
When there wasn't even any Hollywood
They heard the call
And they wrote it on the wall
For you and me we understood

Can it be this sad design
Could be the very same
A wooly man without a face
And a beast without a name
Nothin' here but history
Can you see what has been done
Memory rush over me
Now I step into the sun

Before the fall when they wrote it on the wall
When there wasn't even any Hollywood
They heard the call
And they wrote it on the wall
For you and me we understood

Before the fall when they wrote it on the wall
When there wasn't even any Hollywood
They heard the call
And they wrote it on the wall
For you and me we understood

When Alec completed the song, he looked over at Victor. His expression was priceless and suddenly the middle-aged man looked much younger. With a youthful voice, Victor admitted, "I remember that song from my youth, and the composer got it right. Humans, past and present, always need to express themselves!"

Over the remaining two hours, Benjamin continued to show the coach passengers his island. From Arikok National Park, the tour group was transported to Lourdes Grotto, a shrine built into a hill and then to Casibari Rock Formations, an ancient site with huge monolithic boulders.

By the time they reached the Californian Lighthouse, it had begun to get dark, The lighthouse was known to be the tallest structure in Aruba and had gotten its name from the S.S. *California*, a British steamship that sank off the coast in 1891. That tragedy was the impetus to build a lighthouse.

Alec learned a great deal about Victor during the drive back to the port. Victor's wife, Laura, had worked with Aaron Sloane on several of his ventures. She was also a good friend to Sloane's deceased wife, Lena.

When Alec asked more about his family, Victor confessed, "Laura hasn't been able to travel for some time. She has a crippling form of arthritis. Even though she's housebound, Laura has kept up with important archaeological news. Currently, she's working on a children's book about the subject."

Alec could see that he was immensely proud of both his wife and daughter. Upon asking him which excursion he signed up for in Curaçao, Victor admitted, "I was planning to go to Hato Caves tomorrow, but frankly, I've had enough of rocks to last me the rest of the year."

Not certain he was being serious, Alec just nodded.

The coach returned to the cruise port at seven thirty. Since Paige had sat with Jen during half of the tour, he wanted to hear everything she'd told her. Alec was hungry and Paige wanted to wash away the salt spray and cave dust that had accumulated on her body.

Once aboard the ship, the pair separated. She headed for their cabin and Alec to the Lido Buffet to pick up two meals. By the time he returned to their suite, Paige was out of the tub and ready to have dinner.

While having grilled salmon, wild rice, and asparagus, the DunBartons discussed what each of them learned about their suspects. Paige was full of information about Jennifer Bristow, She discovered that the young woman liked Michael Donovan. Jen hoped that her father would eventually warm up to him.

Alec agreed. "It seems Michael is also taken with her. What was Jen's opinion of Sloane. I heard her once say that he gave her the creeps."

"More than the creeps," Paige laughed. "Jen said that Sloane's 'beady little eyes' used to follow her around a room. On several occasions, he found ways to touch her, sometimes not so innocently."

"Did you get anything else from her?" Alec posed.

Paige, finishing up her rice dish, sighed, "Not really. Just that Annette Perkins could be pushy and Marshall Weissman, pretty sweet."

While stacking up the plates, Paige said, "I have a full day of work tomorrow. What are your plans?"

Alec checked the ship's intranet on his cell phone and complained, "Most of the excursions depart early in the morning. I don't think our archaeologists are beachgoers or want to swim with the dolphins. I'll probably go on the "Discover Curaçao" tour. It visits a museum, another cave, and the Curaçao liquor factory. I wouldn't mind sampling a few of their products."

Less enthusiastically, Alec added, "It leaves at the ungodly hour of 7:30 AM."

Paige commiserated. "In that case, you'd better book the trip now, take a shower, and meet me in bed. I want to watch an old movie on tv."

Alec did what he was told. When he emerged from the bathroom, wrapped in a terrycloth robe, the room's phone rang. Douglas was at the other end, confirming he had mailed the package to Fort Lauderdale from FedEx and sent McGill the tracking number. After a brief conversation, Alec arranged to meet him for lunch the following day.

Paige was in bed and had just started watching *The Mummy*, an old movie with Brendan Fraser.

After setting his alarm for six thirty, Alec joined his wife.

Even though he had seen the film before, Alec had a newfound understanding of how archaeologists saw the world. Alec fell asleep dreaming of fruit bats and creepy crawly insects.

CHAPTER SEVEN

—————————▼—————————

"Lemon Tree"
Words & Music by Will Holt
Genre: Folk, Released: March 1970

Thursday Morning—8th of February

Alec's phone alarm went off as expected at six thirty. Paige was cuddled up against him. Her strawberry blonde hair was disheveled and spread on her pillow. Alec hated to disengage himself from his wife and tried to get out of bed without disturbing her.

Paige woke up long enough to ask him if he was okay. After placing a kiss on her forehead, he urged, "Go back to sleep, Lass."

She turned to her side with a sigh as Alec stepped into the bathroom to get ready for the day. After quickly shaving and dressing, Alec grabbed two buttered rolls, left over from dinner, and managed to leave the cabin by seven.

Alec disembarked the ship hoping to learn something about another FAO member. He wasn't disappointed. In line for the "Discover Curaçao" bus, Alec caught up with Emily Irving. She was alone and Alec immediately engaged her in conversation.

They were still talking when they boarded the bus and Alec took the seat beside her. Emily was not what he'd expected. Alec had assumed that biblical archaeologists were haughty and not very sociable. Instead, he found her delightful. She was full of life and when she laughed, her eyes twinkled in merriment.

Once the bus was full, a middle-aged tour guide stood up and introduced herself. With a Spanish accent, she explained, "My name is Bella. This morning, we're going to visit Hato Caves, the Curaçao Museum, and Chobolobo, the colonial country estate where the famous Curaçao liquor was and is distilled."

Alec and Emily listened to her as she talked about the island's history and culture. She pointed out brightly colored houses in orange, pink, yellow, and purple. Some were beautifully restored while others less so.

The Queen Emma Pontoon Bridge was especially eye catching as it gently swayed in the water. To locals, it was known as the Swinging Old Lady. Bella relayed, "The bridge was opened in 1888 and renovated many times. Originally, pedestrians with shoes were charged two cents to cross it. Those without footwear didn't have to pay. You can imagine that many who could afford shoes went shoeless."

Although the climates of Aruba and Curaçao were very similar, Alec thought the capital city of Willemstad appeared greener than Oranjestad. There were more flowering plants and shade trees along the road. Curaçao seemed a lot less touristy, too.

The drive to Hato Caves didn't take long. Like Guadirikiri Cave in Aruba, the tour group had to navigate many steps to get to the grotto. The cave was full of stalactites and stalagmites that were made to look more eerie by the use of tinted lighting.

The guide pointed out a pirate's head, a sea turtle, and a giant. There were also a few crystal-clear pools and a waterfall. Unfortunately, bats lived in several of the cave's dark recesses.

When a few of the creatures darted out of a hiding place, Emily cried out and grabbed hold of Alec's arm. Afterward, she stayed close to him as they travelled deeper into the cave and ambled up and down stone steps that were dimly lit.

The grounds around Hato Cave included a cactus garden, a few caged animals, and a bar selling souvenirs and cold drinks. Alec, always a gentleman, purchased bottled water for himself and one for Emily. Since the other bus passengers were using the public toilets, the two sat down at a shaded table.

Curious as to what she thought about her fellow archaeologists, Alec invited her to share her thoughts. Emily smiled while talking about the Bristows and said. "Jen is a darling. She has shown the most interest in my work as a biblical archaeologist."

In response, Alec asked whether her field was controversial, and she admitted, "It can be. We haven't been able to confirm as many of the Old Testament stories as we'd like. For example, biblical archaeologists don't know what happened between David and Goliath. We can, however, confirm that David was a real person, and that the Jews and the Philistines lived in the right place, at the right time."

Alec nodded, realizing how difficult it was for her to confirm the thousands of stories in the Bible. Thinking about Goliath's attributes, Alec inquired, "What did you think of Aaron Sloane?"

Turning pale, she replied, "Sloane was a bully and had a way of taking a simple statement and manipulating it into something that no longer represented the truth. A few of his published articles mocked the accomplishments of my coworkers. He was a small, pathetic man."

At that moment, Bella bade her charges to reboard the bus for their second stop.

On the drive to the Curaçao liquor distillery, Alec and Emily continued their conversation. Alec learned that she respected the work of Victor Bristow, and stated, "He has always been accurate in deducing how artifacts were used by indigenous people and fair in concluding how they responded to European rule. Some in my group have not been as honest."

Alec asked whether Sloane was among them. Emily scoffed, "He felt pirates, who lived long enough to enjoy their spoils, survived because they were the fittest. I know he kept about half his valuable finds and used them to gain wealth and power."

When asked about Marshall Weissman and Michael Donovan, she admitted that she didn't know them well. Weissman was always pleasant to her, and Donovan, shy and unassuming. As to Annette Perkins, she proclaimed, "She's a tough cookie and has managed to herd the FAO's cats so far."

Before disembarking at Chobolobo, Alec thanked her for her candor and added, "I'm glad you were able to renew your friendship with my captain. Did you know he had recently transferred to the Pegasus?"

Emily didn't answer. Instead she gave him a Mona Lisa smile that said everything and nothing.

The visit to the distillery proved to be informative and fun. The coach passengers scattered upon entering the air-conditioned building. They were encouraged to look at the exhibits at their own pace. Noting that Emily was somewhere behind him, Alec stepped up to one sign and read:

The island's earliest remains date back to 2,400 BC. It was settled in AD 600 by a branch of Arawak Indians, who canoed over from South America. The Spanish discovered Curaçao in 1499 and later planted Valencia oranges, hoping they would grow on the sunny island. The dry climate caused the tree to wither and it's sweet fruit to become bitter and inedible.

On his way to the next set of signs, Alec burst into song,

When I was just a lad of ten, my father said to me
Come here and take a lesson from the lovely lemon tree
Don't put your faith in love, my boy, my father said to me
I fear you'll find that love is like the lovely lemon tree."

Lemon tree very pretty and the lemon flower is sweet
but the fruit of the poor lemon is impossible to eat
Lemon tree very pretty and the lemon flower is sweet
but the fruit of the poor lemon is impossible to eat

One day beneath the lemon tree, my love and I did lie
A girl so sweet that when she smiled the stars rose in the sky

We passed that summer lost in love beneath the lemon tree
the music of her laughter hid my father's words from me

Lemon tree very pretty and the lemon flower is sweet
but the fruit of the poor lemon is impossible to eat
Lemon tree very pretty and the lemon flower is sweet
but the fruit of the poor lemon is impossible to eat

One day she left without a word. She took away the sun
And in the dark she left behind, I knew what she had done
She'd left me for another, it's a common tale but true
A sadder man but wiser now I sing these words to you

Lemon tree very pretty and the lemon flower is sweet
but the fruit of the poor lemon is impossible to eat
Lemon tree very pretty and the lemon flower is sweet
but the fruit of the poor lemon is impossible to eat

The lyrics prompted Alec to ask himself whether Sloane or his killer was hurt by a beautiful woman. Despite a few stares from people around him, Alec headed over to another placard about the Senior family. It read:

The Senior family's history can be traced back to the fifteenth century Spain. Some of them were *Marranos*—Jews who converted to Christianity to escape persecution during the Spanish Inquisition but secretly practiced Judaism. A few family members immigrated to Curaçao in the 1600s. One of those descendants, Edgar Senior, took the oil from bitter orange peel and mixed it with various exotic spices to create genuine Curaçao Liqueur. In 1896, Edgar Senior founded Senior and Co.

Alec checked out the remaining exhibits but found it impossible to concentrate as he neared the outdoor tasting area. The original orange flavor, coffee, and tamarind were being offered. After tasting each twice, Alec decided the coffee was the most to his liking.

To exit the tasting area, the group had to go through the gift shop. It was there that Alec caught up with Emily. She gave him a shy smile after paying for a couple of small bottles of liqueur.

Back on the coach, Emily explained to Alec, "Several of my contemporaries think it's sinful to drink, but I find a glass of wine with dinner or a cocktail at a party is fine. Wine was commonly imbibed during biblical times in the Middle East and contained less alcohol than it does today. It's also believed that the water had contained harmful microbes and wasn't safe to drink."

Alec nodded, not wanting to tell her that his favorite drink was single-malt Scotch whisky and he sometimes had more than one a day. Together, they agreed that it was wrong to get drunk. Alec especially felt that whisky should be enjoyed, and people who guzzled it down indiscriminately were uncivilized.

The last stop on the tour was Curaçao Museum. Alec found it a bit boring compared to the first two stops on the tour. The museum was housed in a colonial-style building dating back to the 1800s. Its permanent collection included furniture, maps and charts from the Caribbean region, pre-Columbian Indian artifacts, and mahogany woodwork from the eighteenth and nineteenth centuries.

The coach returned to the port at eleven thirty. After going through security, Emily asked Alec whether he and Paige were going to join the FAO members at the Rainbow Grill that evening. Recalling that that the group was scheduled to have pre-dinner drinks at six in the Constellation Lounge and a meal at seven o'clock, Alec replied, "We'll stop by during the cocktail hour."

Moments later, Alec set off for the infirmary to see if Douglas was ready to join him for lunch. He was in luck. The doctor had just finished seeing his last patient of the morning and was ready to have a bite to eat.

The pair ordered cheeseburgers and fries at the Dive In and found a shaded table to have their meal. Alec told him about all the sights he saw and what he and Emily talked about. When he mentioned that he really enjoyed her company, Douglas cautioned, "Don't let Paige or the captain hear you say that!"

Alec laughed. "Now, I can understand what Captain Stewart sees in Emily. She'd better not be the one who poisoned Sloane. So far, it looks like she held the greatest contempt for him."

"I'm glad I'm not in your shoes," Douglas sighed. "You'd better be very sure of your facts when you determine who murdered Sloane."

Alec agreed and left minutes later to check his email. He was eager to see whether McGill had replied to him.

From the Lido Deck, Alec took the elevator to his office. Regina was at her desk when Alec took a seat behind his computer. After a quick exchange, Alec opened his email and was relieved to see a response from Dan McGill at the Fort Lauderdale Homicide Department. It read:

Subj: Florida Archaeologists
Date: 8th of February, 10:50:04 AM EST
From: Dan.McGill@coflso.net
To: AlecDunBarton@aol.com

Alec,

You are a pain in the butt! I have never met a man who attracts murderers the way you do. I received your package this morning. My lab team rushed the tests and have confirmed that the fentanyl in the full bottle of nasal spray was extremely concentrated.

The fentanyl sample contained a large number of contaminants and was likely purchased on the street in pill form. It was strong enough to kill him ten times over. I doubt your doctor would have been able to revive Aaron Sloane with Narcan. His bloodwork showed no other toxins and he was fairly healthy for his age.

I'm not surprised Aaron Sloane met with a violent death. He had some rap sheet. Other than being accused of looting historical treasures from the USA and several foreign countries, Panamanian officials considered him a person of interest when his wife, Lena Sloane, died five years ago today.

At that time, the police received an anonymous call stating that Sloane was slow to get his wife to the hospital. The caller said that Lena had asked for a divorce and had feared for her life. She only permitted him to join her on the dig because she was being accompanied by a few college students and a film crew that was going to take pre-production stills and videos of the area.

The officer in charge of the investigation, Jorge Pino, tried to track down the anonymous caller. Even though he had a tape recording of the message, he was unable to determine whether it was left by a male or a female. He also spoke to the archaeology students who were on the dig with Aaron and Lena and later contacted the film crew that had left days before her death.

Pino discovered that Lena had a number of loud fights with her husband while they were staying at a local hotel near their dig. With no proof that Sloane purposely prevented his wife from getting the urgent medical care she needed, Pino let him return to the United States.

I've learned that Sloane has a large home in Key West, one in Maine, and a condo in Miami Beach. His boat, *The Sultry Siren*, sleeps four to six and is currently moored in the Keys. He has used the boat for many of his archaeological expeditions in the Caribbean. Sloane didn't have children and my team located his brother, Franklin Sloane, in Tampa. Upon informing him of Aaron's death, Frank merely quipped. "He had a good run while it lasted."

I plan to look into Franklin's finances and search for other family members while you interview his colleagues on the Pegasus. It's possible that Aaron's brother gave him the poisoned sinus medicine before he left for the cruise. If he's been named in his brother's will, he could stand to inherit upwards of ten million. People have been murdered for a lot less.

As to the FAO members, I'm still looking into their pasts and whether any of them have used illicit drugs. The only one with a criminal record, other than minor infractions, was Annette Perkins. She was arrested for preventing a builder and his workers from clearing land she felt contained rare Native American relics. Perkins' Cultural Resource team was unable to stop the builder and his well-heeled speculators. After she was arrested, the charges were dropped. Instead of being disgraced, she was later promoted to a higher position within the state government.

That's it for now. Keep me posted.
Dan

While Alec printed out the email, Regina gazed at him with a speculative smile Trying to see what was on the paper, she asked, "So what did Dan McGill have to say?"

Knowing it was useless to keep anything from his shrewd assistant, Alec brought her up to date. Though Alec had read earlier that Lena Sloane had died from a snake bite, he had no idea that Panamanian officials had suspected Aaron of killing her.

Instead of responding to Alec's concerns, Regina declared, "I wonder why Sloane named his boat, *The Sultry Siren*. If it was for his wife, you need to learn more about her and their marriage."

Alec nodded. "I've heard, while Lena Sloane was considered a knowledgeable archaeologist, she was also a femme fatale. You're right, I have to find out who she seduced and how her husband felt about it."

Eager to continue his investigation, Alec rose and headed to the office door.

When Regina inquired where he was going, Alec winked. "I'm going to do some serious sleuthing with Paige tonight."

CHAPTER EIGHT

▼

"On and On"

Words & Music by Stephen Bishop
Genre: Soft Rock, Released: May 1977

Thursday Evening—8th of February

Alec and Paige had a half hour to get ready for the FAO cocktail party at the Constellation Lounge. While Paige was applying makeup, Alec relayed what Dan McGill had written in his email.

When Alec remarked that Sloane may have delayed in getting his wife medical care, Paige nearly stabbed her eye with the mascara brush. Turning to Alec, she exclaimed, "What a horrible man. I understand snake bites can be excruciatingly painful. If he let her die on purpose, he deserved what he got!"

Alec agreed and resumed, "We need to learn more about Lena Sloane. I heard she was pretty close to Emily. It's your job tonight to speak to the biblical archaeologist and find out what Lena's marriage was like and whether she ever cheated on Aaron."

Paige winked. "That's an easy mission. What are you going to do?"

Alec, buttoning up his newly pressed shirt, replied, "I'm going to talk to the men and discover who had the hots for Sloane's wife."

Minutes later, the DunBartons set off for the elevator.

The cocktail party for the archaeologists was sectioned off. Alec greeted Annette, who seemed less than pleased to see him. Shrugging off her scowl, Alec said sweetly, "Thank you for letting us join you."

On seeing Emily seated by a window, Paige rushed ahead of Alec. Alec was steps behind her and called, "I'll get you a gin and tonic."

When Alec returned from the bar, Paige was deep in conversation with Emily Irving. Alec interrupted them for a moment to hand Paige her drink and left wondering how many of the ten commandments Lena Sloane may have broken.

Alec didn't have much time to consider them. Upon seeing Marshall holding a drink and scarfing down a number of warm appetizers from a server. Alec approached him.

Taking a stuffed mushroom from the platter, Alec said, "I understand you were good friends with Aaron Sloane and his wife, Lena. I'd like to know more about them."

Marshall's eyes lit up when Alec pointed to a vacant table and invited, "Let's take a seat."

Once they were settled, Weissman asked, "So, what do you want to know?"

Alec began, "How long did you work for Sloane?"

Weissman paused before answering. "About ten years, on and off. He liked to use my scientific expertise to find places to dig on land and at sea."

When Alec inquired about Marshall's relationship with Lena, the nerdy tech actually blushed. To hide his reaction, he took a sip of his drink and began to choke. Alec waited until he could talk and was surprised to hear that the two of them had a short affair.

Alec urged Weissman to tell him more.

Marshall admitted, "We got involved about six months before her death. It was after she broke up with Victor Bristow. She told me she wanted to have children and that Sloane was adamantly against it. While I was trying to comfort her, one thing led to another. We were alone on the yacht at the time."

Weissman blushed again and then announced, "She was a beautiful woman, full of life. She had so much to give. It's a shame she went on that dig in Panama. If I had been with her, that *snake* would have never gotten near her."

Not sure whether he was talking about Aaron Sloane or a reptile, Alec asked, "Did it bother you that Lena had been with other men?"

A flash of anger appeared in Weissman's eyes as he replied, "Like I said, Lena was beautiful. Her husband couldn't give her what she needed. It wasn't her fault she had to look elsewhere."

All too soon, the cocktail hour came to an end. When Annette announced that everyone should make their way down to the Rainbow Grill, Alec sought out Paige. She had just concluded her conversation with Emily.

When the group departed for the reservations-only restaurant, Paige asked, "So, where are we going to have dinner?"

Alec led her to the staircase and replied, "It's seven o'clock. Let's see if we can catch Douglas and Regina at the buffet. I especially want to hear what Emily Irving had to tell you."

Together, they headed to the informal eatery.

While Paige looked for Dr. Abbot and Regina Hill at their favorite table, Alec waited in a line at the carvery for two dishes of roast beef, Yorkshire pudding, and mushy peas. Moments later, Paige caught up with Alec and led him to their friends who were seated near their usual spot and halfway through their meal.

Once they were settled, Regina asked them what they discovered at the cocktail party. Alec, eager to hear what Emily Irving had to say, pressed Paige to reveal what she'd learned.

After taking a sip of iced tea, Paige began, "It was initially hard for me to get Emily to talk. She didn't want to speak ill of the dead.

Lena had been a close friend to her. They attended the same college and majored in archaeology. Both women considered themselves good Christians.

"Lena married when she was in her late twenties to a history professor employed at Florida State University. They were very happy and had a son. When the boy was four years old, he drowned in the family pool. Lena was unable to forgive her husband, who she'd left to watch him. Upon divorcing him, Lena became a different woman. She stopped believing in God and decided to live her life without thought to the consequences."

Paige paused to take another sip of her beverage and then continued. "Emily lost track of Lena for many years and didn't catch up with her again until she remarried. At that time, Lena just seemed interested in money, power, and prestige. Though Aaron and Lena did not have an official open marriage, both of them 'enjoyed' the company of others."

Alec nodded, "I'm getting a better picture of Lena Sloane. The loss of a child can cause a parent to wonder whether there is a God. All of a sudden, your life has little meaning and you have no idea how to go on."

Paige patted Alec's hand. The loss of his wife and daughter to a drunk driver in London had caused him to examine his life. In response to their deaths, he joined the staff of the cruise line to find out who killed the previous controller. If it hadn't been for the friendship of Douglas, Paige, and Regina, Alec might have also given into his worst desires.

Sympathetically, Regina added. "I nearly went off the deep end when my husband died, and I had grown children to keep an eye on me." Addressing Alec, she murmured, "Thank goodness you met Paige."

Alec smiled at his wife and agreed, "She gave me a reason to live again. The same can't be said for Lena."

"As to Lena's lovers," Paige rejoined, "Emily didn't know which men she might have tangled with."

Alec replied, "I know one for certain."

Both Douglas and Regina asked who at the same time.

Alec laughed, "Would you believe Marshall Weissman, the nerdy tech guy?"

Suspiciously, Paige asked, "Are you sure he wasn't making it up?"

Alec shook his head, "I don't think so. Their affair, though short lived, was very important to him. Marshall said he got to know the real Lena, and she let him see her vulnerable side. She wanted to change her life and felt she could give a great deal to a child."

When I asked Weissman about her other beaus, he admitted she had many but could just name Victor Bristow for certain."

Paige exclaimed, "Victor! That man is dry as dust. He only displays emotion when he's with his daughter."

Alec cautioned, "I'll need to speak to Bristow before I can confirm that Lena had an affair with him."

Over dessert and coffee, the foursome continued to talk about Lena and Aaron Sloane. Wondering what women Sloane may have loved and left, Alec sang out,

Down in Jamaica, they got lots of pretty women
Steal your money, then they break your heart
Lonesome Sue, she's in love with old Sam
Take him from the fire into the frying pan

On and on, she just keeps on trying
And she smiles when she feels like crying
On and on, on and on, on and on

Poor old Jimmy sits alone in the moonlight
Saw his woman kiss another man
So he takes a ladder, steals the stars from the sky
Puts on Sinatra and starts to cry

On and on, he just keeps on trying
And he smiles when he feels like crying
On and on, on and on, on and on

When the first time is the last time

It can make you feel so bad
But if you know it, show it
Hold on tight, don't let her say goodnight

Got the sun on my shoulders and my toes in the sand
Woman's left me for some other man
Aw, but I don't care, I'll just dream and stay tanned
Toss up my heart and see where it lands

On and on, I just keep on trying
And I smile when I feel like dying
On and on, on and on, on and on
On and on, on and on, on and on
On and on, on and on, on and on

At 9:00 PM, Paige warned Alec, "We'd better get going. The servers are eager to clean up, and I have a full day tomorrow."

When they disbanded near the elevator, Douglas agreed to join Alec at the second archaeology talk the following afternoon. Before that, Alec hoped to have a private conversation with Victor Bristow. With those plans made, Alec and Paige departed for their cabin.

Like most evenings, Paige headed to the bathroom to fill the tub with bath gel. Uncertain he'd be sleepy enough by bedtime, Alec gave Paige a kiss and said, "I'm going to take a walk around the Promenade Deck to sort out everything I heard tonight."

Paige assured him, "I'll be here when you get back. Just don't take too long!"

Eager to go and now return, he promised, "I'll be back soon."

Alec circled the deck several times and returned to the cabin still feeling unsettled. Paige was already in bed and beckoned, "If you want to cuddle, don't dally. I'm getting pretty sleepy."

That's all Alec had to hear to drive all thoughts of the FAO members from his mind.

After getting in beside Paige, Alec muttered, "Your feet are cold. Is there any other place that needs my attention?"

Paige merely smiled.

Alec did not want to get out of bed the next morning. Before leaving for the Future Cruise Desk, Paige left a cup of piping hot coffee on Alec's bedside table along with three mini muffins. While Alec enjoyed his breakfast, he thought for the umpteenth time that life was good.

It took some effort for him to finally shower, shave, and dress. Though the DunBartons did not use the daily services of a room steward, Alec was happy to let Bakti into the room to replace the towels and take away dirty dishes.

Leaving Bakti to tidy up, Alec headed to the Hudson Room where the Florida archaeologists were scheduled to meet from ten to eleven. It was 9:40 AM when he entered the lounge.

On top of the bar, the server had set up a platter of fresh fruit, assorted cheeses, and breakfast breads. Despite eating everything that Paige had left him, Alec helped himself to some cheese and cut-up melon.

There were only a few members milling about the room. Alec spoke to several of them, asking them how they were enjoying themselves and what they had seen in Curaçao. Several of them expressed a keen interest in visiting Cartagena, Columbia, the following day.

The relaxed atmosphere in the lounge changed when Annette Perkins entered the room. She was unpleasant to Alec and immediately complained that he was attending too many of the FAO functions.

Smiling to hide his anger, Alec pulled her aside and said in a menacing tone, "Expect me to be at *all* of them. It's very unlikely that a complete stranger murdered Aaron Sloane. One of your members killed him, and I plan to interview every one of them until I complete my investigation. Have I made myself clear?"

Annette's plump face turned bright red, and she merely nodded. Her expression reminded Alec of a bull dog who was scolded by its owner for soiling the carpet.

When everyone was seated, Annette announced, "We're holding our second archaeological lecture today in the Starlight Lounge. I had arranged for Aaron Sloane to conduct it. As he passed away, I've asked Michael, our underwater archaeologist, and Victor, our European exploration expert to lead the talk. It's going to be called, 'Tale of Two Pirates.'

"As arranged," she continued, "Marshall will fill in with the technical info, and I will make sure the audio-visual equipment is set up properly. Does anyone have questions?"

Several hands went up. One person wanted to know what they were going to entitle their third lecture. Annette listened to several suggestions. After a short round of voting, the group decided to call it, "Mankind Through the Ages."

With that settled, Annette adjourned the meeting so that Victor, Michael, and Marshall could go over what they wanted to discuss at their seminar. Though Alec would have liked to have a tête-à-tête with Bristow then and there, he made arrangements to meet him for afternoon tea at three o'clock.

Unable to get anything else done, Alec visited his office. Regina's spreadsheets needed to be double checked for accuracy. For the next two hours, Alec looked over her revenue reports.

At one o'clock, Alec stopped off at the Lido Buffet to pick up a Rueben sandwich, potato chips, and iced tea. He had to rush to meet Douglas in the right-hand wing of the Starlight Lounge on the Promenade Deck.

Upon entering the large auditorium, Alec noted there were many more passengers seated in the audience than at the FAO's first talk. After finding two seats, Alec whispered to Douglas, "I guess passengers are interested in pirates and their booty."

The program started when Faith approached the microphone and announced, "I see our archaeology classes are becoming very popular. Today, you're in for a treat. Victor Bristow is going to speak first and tell you about the four European powers that created colonies in the new world.

Victor looked at ease as he introduced the rest of the panel, which included Michael Donovan and Marshall Weissman. With a handheld clicker, Bristow showed the audience a slide of the East Indies in the 1660s.

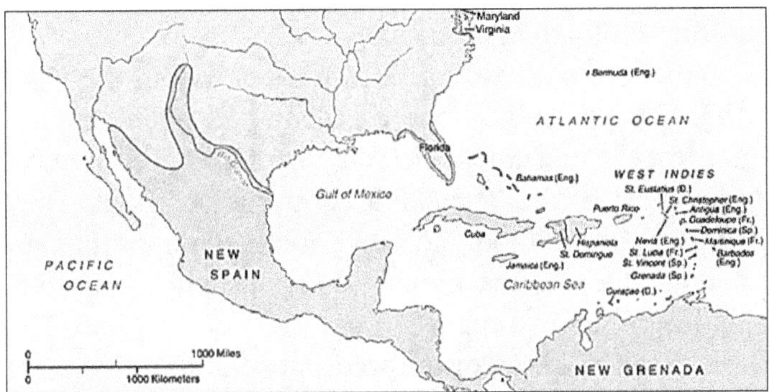

After describing how Spain, France, England, and the Netherlands carved up portions of the New World, Victor clicked on a second slide. It showed the kinds of trade being conducted, the location of Spanish gold and silver mines, and where Henry Morgan and Blackbeard led many of their infamous raids.

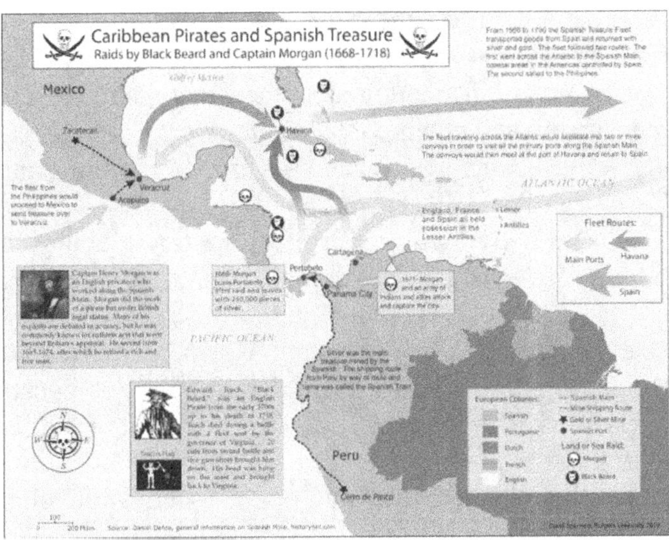

While talking about the image, Bristow clarified, "Pirates were men and women who attacked ships or coastal towns in an attempt to rob them or capture prisoners for ransom. Essentially, they were thieves with a boat. They have been a menace since ancient times, but they were especially ruthless from the 1660s to the 1730s, known as the 'Golden Age of Piracy.'

"It is believed that 2,400 pirates were active in the Caribbean during that time period. Some of them had been employed as sailors and others had left their war-torn nations to begin a new trade in the West Indies. Pirates rarely possessed gold. They stole items like tools, rope, food, clothing, and general merchant cargo. If they managed to acquire money, it was usually spent in port on gambling, liquor, and women.

"Unlike pirates who worked solely for themselves, there were also privateers, employed by a country to fight the nation's enemies. They had official sanction to destroy ships, take cargo, and keep a portion of the plunder. A buccaneer, a French term, refers to a pirate or privateer that was active in the late 1600s."

To make the point, Victor displayed a grisly illustrated slide of Edward Teach aka Blackbeard. He explained, "Blackbeard had been a privateer for the British during the War of the Spanish Succession between 1701 and 1713.

"From 1714 to 1718, he went into business for himself. Blackbeard converted a captured French merchant vessel into a forty-gun warship and renamed it *Queen Anne's Revenge*. He often raided the Virginia and Carolina coasts and looted ships and ports in the Caribbean Sea.

"Blackbeard had a base in a North Carolina inlet and forcibly collected tolls from ships in Pamlico Sound. At the request of Carolina planters, the lieutenant governor of Virginia dispatched a British naval force under Lieutenant Robert Maynard. After a bloody fight, Blackbeard was killed. The pirate was decapitated, and his head was affixed to the end of the bowsprit of the ship as a warning to other pirates."

Bristow then handed the microphone and slide clicker to Michael Donovan. Uncertain whether the young man was used to public speaking, Alec turned to Douglas and muttered, "He looks nervous."

As Donovan spoke, his voice became stronger. Decisively, he explained, "On the ninth of January in 1671, Captain Henry Morgan and his men sailed up the Chagres River on the Atlantic Coast side of Panama. Their mission was to pillage and loot Panama City on the Pacific Coast. At that time, five of Morgan's ships sank on the treacherous Lajas Reef. Despite losing his flagship, *The Satisfaction*, the privateers continued their fifteen-mile trek, through rivers and dense rainforest, to get to their destination.

"Captain Morgan was successful in his mission. His forces were met by approximately 1,200 Spanish infantry and 400 cavalry men. During their primary battle, over 400 Spanish soldiers died in comparison to fifteen privateers. Morgan and his men spent three weeks in Panama City, plundering what they could after much of the town was set on fire."

Michael stopped to show a slide of him in a group photo with other underwater archeologists and explained, "I was fortunate to be part of a team that unearthed Henry Morgan's flagship, *The Satisfaction*. It had been buried since 1671 and discovered in 2011 when two inches of the hull was found sticking out of the seabed. After excavating it from mud and clay, we found several wooden chests, guns, and six cannons. Because archaeologists do not keep their finds, it was given to the Panama National Institute of Culture."

While Donovan showed pictures of those artifacts, he told the audience that Henry Morgan, unlike Blackbeard, remained a privateer with the British government. Although he sometimes went on raids in which he had no legal justification, he shared his plunder with England for thirty years. He lived out his days in Port Royal, Jamaica, a rich and respected man.

Marshall spoke next and talked about equipment that archeologists depended upon to find shipwrecks. With enthusiasm, he described how magnetometers use magnetism to locate metal objects underwater and how it was instrumental in locating *The*

Satisfaction. After delineating how two hundred-to-nine-hundred-pound cannons were lifted off the reef and moved to land, Marshall handed the microphone to Faith.

She brought the lecture to a close by thanking the speakers and reminding passengers that the ship's shop had books on famous pirates and other seafaring items for sale.

As the audience filed out of the lounge to go to their next activity, Alec gazed at his watch. It was 2:50 PM. Though he expected that Victor Bristow might be late in meeting him for afternoon tea at three, Alec said goodbye to Douglas.

As the two men parted, "Dr. Abbot said, "Let me know whether Bristow behaved like a pirate or privateer when he had an affair with Lena Sloane."

Alec winked, "From what I've heard about Lena, I wouldn't be surprised if she took her cues from Blackbeard."

CHAPTER NINE

▼

"Addicted to Love"
Words & Music by Robert Palmer
Genre: Rock, Released: January 1986

Friday Afternoon—9th of February

Alec had to wait a few minutes for Victor Bristow to show up for afternoon tea at the Brittania Dining Room. He apologized for being late and appeared unsettled. There were cracks in his poker face and he appeared drained.

The maître d took the two men to a table for two that overlooked the ocean. Trying to dispel the tension, Alec complimented, "I loved your presentation, especially the historic facts that led to the Golden Age of Piracy. It's a fascinating subject."

As the waiter filled their teacups and placed a three-tier cake stand on the white tablecloth, Victor spoke up. "I believe you have other things on your mind. What did you want to talk to me about?"

Taking a quarter of a cream cheese and smoked salmon sandwich, Alec said, "I want to know about you and Lena Sloane. I heard you two had a relationship."

Bristow scowled. "Marshall has a big mouth." Taking a slight pause, he added, "It was a big mistake. I realized it soon after we made love for the first time."

Alec wondered why he used the term *made love* when he could have said "had sex" or "got together." Uncertain whether Victor had fallen in love with Sloane's wife, Alec asked him to go on.

As the archaeologist spoke, Alec learned that Lena had been good friends with Victor and his wife, Laura, for over twenty years. On several occasions the two couples travelled together and frequently spent time on Aaron's yacht. They had originally met at an archaeology conference in Salzburg, Austria. Since they both lived in Florida and had mutual friends, it was easy for them to mingle.

Getting to the heart of the matter, Victor confided, "Laura's arthritis has worsened over the last few years and when it became clear that her travelling days were over, Lena made sexual overtures to me. At first, I felt flattered and laughed it off. Instead of putting her off, it seemed to encourage her.

"Lena was not only a seductive woman, but also beautiful and talented. I'm ashamed to say, I took the path of least resistance and had an affair with her. For me it was more than a fling. We met whenever we could at hotels and out of the way places. It lasted about a year and ended six months before Lena passed away. During that time, I lied to Laura and paid little attention to Jen. I still don't know how I became so enraptured by her. It was like an addiction."

That's all Alec had to hear before singing out,

Your lights are on, but you're not home
Your mind is not your own
Your heart sweats, your body shakes
Another kiss is what it takes
You can't sleep, you can't eat
There's no doubt, you're in deep
Your throat is tight, you can't breathe
Another kiss is all you need
Ohh oohh

You like to think that you're immune to the stuff...oh yeah
It's closer to the truth to say you can't get enough
You know you're gonna have to face it
You're addicted to love

You see the signs, but you can't read
You're runnin' at a different speed
You heart beats in double time
Another kiss and you'll be mine, a one-track mind
You can't be saved
Oblivion is all you crave
If there's some left for you
You don't mind if you do
Ohh oohh

You like to think that you're immune to the stuff
It's closer to the truth to say you can't get enough
You know you're gonna have to face it
You're addicted to love

Might as well face it, you're addicted to love
Might as well face it, you're addicted to love
Might as well face it, you're addicted to love
Might as well face it, you're addicted to love
Might as well face it, you're addicted to love

Victor looked around the dining room to see if anyone else heard Alec's rendition of the Robert Palmer song. This time Victor was *not* amused and made a move to leave the table.

Still needing some questions answered, Alec apologized for his poor timing and got Bristow to remain sitting. When he inquired whether Aaron ever learned of his affair with Lena, Victor nodded. "He didn't care and said, 'It was best to keep it in the family.'" Starring at Alec, he asked, "What the hell did that mean?"

Alec was equally puzzled and inquired whether his relationship with Sloane had changed afterward. Victor merely shrugged, "We remained friendly, but it never returned to how it was. Lena's death hit me hard, and Aaron seemed to get over it within months."

When the servers began to clear the table, Alec got to his final question and asked, "Do you have any idea who might have killed Aaron Sloane?"

As he rose to leave, Bristow replied, "Sloane made lots of enemies over his lifetime. His business associates didn't trust him and he could be an egotistical son of a bitch. It could have been anybody."

With that said, he departed.

Alec's next task was to locate Annette Perkins, He tracked her down at the Lido Bar with Jen Bristow having the drink of the day—a Coco Loco with fruit juice, coconut cream, and rum.

Eager to learn what they were going to do in Cartagena, Columbia, the following day, Alec asked if he could join them. Jen's dimples creased in joy as she patted the chair beside her.

Before Alec could bring up the subject, Jen posed, "Annette and I want to know whether it's safe to go on an excursion in Cartagena. We've heard that passengers have been drugged or worse. Is it true?"

Alec nodded, "In the past, Columbia was considered a dangerous place for tourists to visit. Some cruise lines had removed the port of call from their itineraries. The area is much safer now. You should be fine in your tour group. Just don't wander off by yourself or take anything, including flyers, from strangers."

Jen laughed. "You sound like my father. I may sit out the stop. The shore excursions leave really early, and I'd like to stay up late at the ship's barbecue and moonlight dance."

Alec smiled seeing her youthful exuberance and asked Annette about her plans. She replied, "I'm going on a walking tour of the walled city with a few other members. I've always been fascinated with the city since seeing *Romancing the Stone*. The movie spurred my interest in archaeology. It was only later, I learned that the famous scene with the alligators was really filmed at the San Juan de Ulúa Castle in Veracruz, Mexico."

"It's going to be hot and humid in town," Jen reminded. "Make sure you wear sunscreen and drink plenty of water."

Annette patted the young woman's hand affectionately, and Alec found himself reevaluating Perkins. She didn't seem as dogged as she first seemed. Deciding to learn more about her at another time, Alec said, "Paige and I plan to have dinner at the Columbia barbeque, too. Perhaps we'll see you later."

As Alec walked away from the pair, he heard Jen giggle and say, "He's very handsome. Don't you agree?"

Alec wasn't able to make out Perkins' reply.

Despite the heat of the day, the Lido Deck felt cool, and the tropical breezes enhanced the sensation. The stands for food were attractively decorated and were arranged around the pool. In one corner of the deck was a calypso band showcasing rhythmic and harmonious vocals. The evening felt magical.

Alec kissed Paige as they took in their surroundings. He had managed to pull his wife away from her desk an hour early. She just had time to freshen up and slip on a flowery sundress before he hurried her up to the barbeque.

Paige smiled. "I'm glad you insisted I come. I can't believe we missed this event when we previously sailed to Cartagena."

Spotting an empty table for four near the Lido Bar, Alec urged, "Let's grab those seats before we check out the Columbian cuisine."

Paige had to rush to keep up with Alec's long strides and arrived at the table as another couple reached it. When Paige looked up at their faces, she nudged Alec, "Look who's here."

Alec was thrilled to see Michael Donovan with Jennifer Bristow and said, "We must share the table."

Jen graciously agreed and replied, "It looks like the Lido Deck is going to get very crowded. We'd love to join you."

Michael looked a little less pleased but must have noticed there were no empty tables for two. After he pulled out the chair for Jen, he remained standing and asked everyone, "What can I get you to drink at the bar?"

Jen wanted another Coco Loco, remarking, "I think they're addictive."

Alec refrained from singing, "Addicted to Love," this time but wondered what else the young woman found habit forming. Michael was certainly attractive with his athletically tanned body and expressive brown eyes.

Donovan left with their drink orders and returned with a server. Alec thanked him when Michael signed the chit for all four beverages and promised to pay for the next round. Jen giggled in response and explained, "This drink is more potent then it looks. I may need some help getting back to my cabin."

Michael appeared to blush in response, and Alec found himself thinking that the fellow was less experienced with women than he'd previously thought. Since Jen was sharing a cabin with Emily and Michael with Marshall, Alec decided that there was little chance for them to spend the night together until after the cruise.

Once the drinks were handed out, Alec suggested, "Why don't you two get something to eat. We'll hold down the table."

Enthusiastically, they rose to see what fare was being offered. While they were gone, Paige remarked, "You couldn't have planned this any better."

Alec grinned. "I was hoping to speak to them individually, but it should be interesting to see how they both react to certain questions."

Paige warned, "Just don't be mean. They both seem so young and innocent."

Alec nodded, not sure what he was going to ask.

Five minutes later, the twosome returned. Michael's plate was laden with all sorts of food and Alec's estimation of Donovan grew. Alec felt a man with a good appetite had little to hide. That clue to a person's character did not work as well on women. They always seemed to be dieting.

Michael showed Alec everything he had picked up from the food stands. He explained, "The server said that Columbians sell barbequed meats on the streets, known as *fritanga*. I have flank steak with salsa, beef ribs, chorizo, pork sausage, chicken with rice, and fried plantains."

Alec's mouth started to water, and he quickly excused Paige and himself to get their meals. When they returned, his plate looked very similar to Donovan's. Paige had a few of the same items but doubled up on arepas, a kind of corn bread stuffed with braised beef.

Over their meal, the foursome conversed about a wide range of topics. Both of them had only nice things to say about Annette Perkins. When she took over from Aaron Sloane, she whipped the organization into shape by responding to emails promptly, sending newsletters on time, and arranging the cruise. Under Sloane, there were always issues due to miscommunication.

On the subject of Sloane, Jen confirmed that when she was young, she and her parents had gone on several trips with Aaron and Lena. She remembered them fondly and, at the time, Aaron always made her feel like one of his family. He often gave her gifts and treated her like a daughter. Since the Sloanes didn't have children of their own, she accepted his attention. It became uncomfortable after Lena died.

Upon asking Donovan whether he ever made the acquaintance of Lena Sloane, the fellow blushed again, Michael replied shyly that she had been on a few of her husband's sea voyages and had been a bit *too* friendly.

Earnestly, he added, "I let her know I wasn't interested. After a few attempts, she gave up."

Jen laughed, "Lena could be a real handful. I guess I shouldn't be surprised she tried it out on Michael. Lena was very nice but also very lonely. She lost her son when he was a toddler. I think she had hoped to fill the hole in her heart with booze and men. Once, she even tried to seduce my father."

Donovan nearly choked, and Alec had to wonder whether Michael knew of Victor's affair with Lena.

The meal ended all too soon. Before Michael and Jen could depart for a romantic dance in the moonlight, Alec asked, "Who's going into Cartagena tomorrow morning."

With a mischievous smile, Jen recalled, "Annette, my dad, Marshall, Emily, and three other couples. Michael and I plan to relax the entire day."

The dimples in her cheeks creased again as she headed to the makeshift dance floor with Michael.

When they were out of hearing range, Paige exclaimed, "Donovan is a real boy scout. I can't imagine he ever gets into trouble."

Gazing at Jen's retreating figure, he replied, "He may tonight. That young lady can be a *handful*."

Paige smiled. "She might not be the only one. Let's show them how a middle-aged couple dances cheek to cheek."

Alec obediently followed behind his wife.

CHAPTER TEN

▼

"Money, Money, Money"
Words & Music by Benny Andersson and Björn Ulvaeus
Genre: Baroque Pop Rock, Released: November 1976

Saturday Afternoon—10th of February

Alec awakened late in the morning after having a wonderful evening. Since Paige had the morning off, the couple lounged in bed and did not stick their heads out the door until lunchtime. When Paige finally set off for an appointment with a future cruiser, Alec turned on his laptop to see whether there was any word from McGill.

Pleased to see a message in his inbox, Alec placed his second cup of coffee on the desk and opened the email. It read:

Subj: Update on Frankin Sloane
Date: 10th of February, 9:21:11 AM EST
From: Dan.McGill@coflso.net
To: AlecDunBarton@aol.com

Alec,

Last night, I had an interesting conversation with Sloane's brother, Franklin. I asked him whether he knew the contents of his Aaron's will. As his executor, he had a copy of it and believes it was the last one his brother wrote. Prior to that period, Lena was his main beneficiary with some small bequests and treasured objects going to friends and museums. Also interesting to note, Lena never signed a prenuptial agreement and had she divorced in Florida, would have received half of his estate.

Although it will take some time before our medical examiner can sign an official death certificate, I asked Franklin if he'd mind sharing the will's contents. He had no issue with my request, hoping it could help solve Aaron's murder. He disclosed to me that he was to receive 50% of his estate with the remaining 50% going to Jennifer Bristow.

Alec nearly knocked the coffee cup off his desk as he read Jen's name. What was she to Aaron Sloane? Did she know she was named in his will? Could she have poisoned him with fentanyl just to get her hands on *his* money?"

With those thoughts on his mind, Alec sang out the chorus of the Abba song,

Money, money, money
Must be funny
In the rich man's world
Money, money, money
Always sunny
In the rich man's world
Aha-aha

All the things I could do
If I had a little money
It's a rich man's world
It's a rich man's world

A man like that is hard to find
But I can't get him off my mind
Ain't it sad?
And if he happens to be free
I bet he wouldn't fancy me
That's too bad

So I must leave, I'll have to go
To Las Vegas or Monaco
And win a fortune in a game
My life will never be the same

Money, money, money
Must be funny
In the rich man's world
Money, money, money
Always sunny
In the rich man's world

Still unsettled, Alec mused, "Did Ms. Bristow cozy up to a rich man even though he was a longtime family friend. Of course, it could have been the other way around. Aaron Sloane might have been fixated on his friend's daughter.

Eagerly, Alec returned to McGill's message and read:

When I asked Franklin what he knew about Jennifer Bristow, he was full of information. Apparently, Sloane had an affair with Laura Bristow about nine months before Jen was born. Victor was away in Europe. Franklin had encouraged his brother to confirm his relationship with Ms. Bristow with a DNA test. Aaron said it was unnecessary and the money should go to her even if she wasn't related by blood. He admitted that Laura Bristow was the only woman he ever loved, and Jen was the daughter he wished he'd had. Franklin let the matter drop.

I looked into Franklin's finances. He's a bigshot in Tampa and appears to be well heeled. I'll keep digging and also find out whether the Bristows were short of cash. I can't imagine that archaeologists, who work for the government, make lots of money. It's possible that Jen, her father, or even Laura Bristow learned about the will and had a hand in rushing along Sloane's death.

Keep me posted.
Dan

Alec reread the email one more time before setting off to find Victor Bristow. The tour of the Old City of Cartagena was scheduled to conclude at one o'clock.

Since it was 1:10 PM, Alec took the stairs to the Main Deck where the security kiosk was scanning passengers on their return to the ship. Alec didn't have to wait long. He spotted Victor on the gangway talking to Emily Irving. When they entered the Pegasus, Bristow complained to Alec, "You're not waiting for me, are you?"

Alec nodded, "I need to speak to you alone!"

The two men found seats in the Bull Dog Pub on the Upper Promenade. The lounge contained leather-upholstered booths with wood and brass decor that was polished with care.

Both of them were thirsty. After ordering cold beers and two ploughman's lunches, Alec began. "I just heard from my police contact in Fort Lauderdale. He has been in touch with Aaron Sloane's brother, Franklin. It has come to our attention that your daughter has been named a 50% beneficiary of Sloane's large estate. Were you aware of that?"

Bristow's placid expression turned into one of shock. Alec deduced that Victor was either an excellent liar or truly shaken. Slowly the surprise turned to acceptance as he uttered, "It makes sense now. Sloane always had a soft spot for Jen. He and Lena never had children."

Not accepting the statement at face value, Alec accused, "It was more than that! Sloane told his brother that he was Jen's biological father, and you were on a dig when your daughter was conceived."

Victor's eyes turned steely gray before saying succinctly, "I may have let that conceited buffoon believe it. Over the years, Aaron took great pleasure in bringing up the past, mentioning that he was there for Laura when I was away. I always knew what he was insinuating. Laura told me about their brief affair soon after it happened.

"Later, Laura had me undergo a DNA test. Jennifer is definitely mine."

Over their meal of cheese, bread, and chutney, Alec learned that Victor's relationship with Aaron was always competitive. Victor felt he was smarter and better educated than his nemesis. Aaron considered wealth and power more important than knowledge. Both men seemed to enjoy their battle of values.

Although, Victor and Aaron differed in personality, both of them had affairs with each other's spouses. Bristow might have seduced Lena for payback. Both claimed to be Jen's father, and both were capable of killing someone to get what they wanted.

It was possible that Aaron murdered his wife to keep her from divorcing him. Victor could have killed Sloane aware that his daughter was going to inherit a fortune. Maybe wealth was more important to Victor than he'd stated.

While having a second round of beers, Alec broached a more sensitive subject and asked, "Does Jen know that Sloane left her money or that he once had an affair with her mother?"

Miserably, Bristow shook his head. "I don't think so. Can you keep it to yourself?"

Alec replied, "You may be able to convince Jen that Sloane left her money because he never had children, but the rest will come out sooner or later. I can't promise she won't hear about it from me. You'd better tell her everything."

Victor heaved a sigh and for the first time Alec felt sorry for him. He didn't want to destroy Bristow's relationship with his daughter.

The two men parted on good terms. Victor left to go to an afternoon meeting in the Churchill Room and Alec to finish some work at his office.

At seven thirty, Alec and Paige met up with Douglas and Regina for drinks at the Lido Bar. Upon bringing everyone up to date on his investigation, Alec asked them about their plans for the following day.

Paige shared, "I have the day off, and Alec and I are going on the 'Shaping of Panama' tour. After the ship passes through the first three canal locks, a boat in Gatun Lake will take us to the shoreline where we'll board an excursion bus for Panama City."

Taking a breath, she continued. "The coach is going to traverse the Trans-Isthmus Highway from the Atlantic to the Pacific. It's the same route that Forty-Niners took to get to the gold fields in California. When we arrive in Panama City, we'll be given lunch and visit Old Panama City, which was destroyed by Henry Morgan in 1671."

Regina gushed, "That sounds wonderful. How long is the tour? I'd love to take it someday but the "walk" in the Spanish Quarter may not be leisurely enough for me."

Dr. Abbot patted Regina's knee. "You're probably wise, my dear." Making a slight joke, he added, "At our age, we should go on the 'Canal Nature Watch.' I understand that three-toed sloths move even slower than us."

Paige smiled at her friend's antics and answered, "The tour takes seven hours and it includes a ninety-minute bus ride each way. I hope our transit through the canal doesn't get delayed. On the last cruise, we had to wait a few hours before we could pass through."

Alec agreed. "The canal seems to get busier every day. I thought there was going to be less traffic when the huge Panamax ship lanes and locks were completed in 2016."

"I'm glad," Paige declared, "that our ship is small enough to navigate through the original locks." Speaking to Regina, Paige asked, "Do you still get up early on the canal days to watch our ship enter the first lock?"

Regina nodded, "I know it should be old hat by now, but it's really amazing what the builder's accomplished in 1914. Besides that, I love the Panama buns that are served in the bow of the ship."

Alec laughed and said, "See! I'm not the only one who likes those peach and cream yeast rolls. They're delicious with black coffee."

Douglas couldn't help commenting, "They're not very healthy and too sweet for my taste."

"You're just an old fuddy duddy," Regina retorted. 'I think it's important to have balance in your life. Enjoy yourself, eat and drink a yummy thing once a day, and be kind to each other."

"Sound advice," Paige agreed.

Alec gazed at his wristwatch a moment later and remarked to Paige, "We'd better not stay up late. The Pegasus is scheduled to go through the Panama Canal around seven o'clock and our tour is supposed to leave at 10:30 AM.

After finishing their drinks, Paige and Alec said their goodbyes and returned to their cabin. Before turning in for the evening, Paige reminded Alec to set his phone alarm.

Alec scowled. "I'd better get up by six thirty. The FAO members plan to meet then to watch the transit from the bow of the Vista Deck."

As Paige lifted up the comforter to get into bed, she murmured, "Oh good. Bring me two Panama buns. I plan to sleep in till 8:30 AM and have them for breakfast."

Alec grumbled in response.

CHAPTER ELEVEN

▼

"Panama"
Words & Music by Eddie Van Halen,
Alec Van Halen, Michael Anthony, and David Lee Roth
Genre: Glam Metal Rock, Released: April 1984

Sunday Morning—11th of February

Alec didn't bother to shave and slipped on the clothes he had worn the night before. He was not a morning person, and he felt miserable as he quietly closed the suite door behind him.

The bow on the Vista Deck was full of activity. Crew members were stationed at the heavy door leading to the bow of the ship. They were present to help passengers step over the six-inch metal lip in the doorway. The ship's personnel didn't want its guests to fall, or worse, take a header into the Panama Canal.

Once on the ship's bow, Alec made a beeline for the peaches and cream Panama buns. After washing one down with a tepid cup of black coffee, Alec looked around.

Annette Perkins was standing on the port side of the open deck facing east. The sun was just rising behind soft white clouds. She barely looked up when Alec approached but seemed to be glad of his company.

In response to Alec's greeting, she admitted, "I've been to some beautiful places in my lifetime but seeing the Panama Canal is a real highlight. Aaron suggested the trip, and it didn't take a lot to convince me that this cruise was going to be perfect for our members."

Alec hadn't known whose idea it was and filed that information away for later. Caught up in her excitement, Alec asked about the others.

Gazing at the majestic Atlantic Bridge spanning the entrance to the Canal, Annette replied, "Many of them should be here shortly. I think Emily is watching from the captain's bridge and some planned to see it from the Lido Deck."

As she uttered those words, Marshall showed up, followed by Jennifer Bristow. Jen announced that her dad was going to be late after having a sleepless night. Moments later, Michael Donovan made an appearance with a milky cup of coffee for Jennifer.

She took it from the young man with gratitude and flashed him one of those smiles that could melt an ice cube. They all had plenty to say about the approach to the first lock of three to Gatun Lake.

When the huge gates of the first chamber began to open, the voice of the cruise director explained over the loudspeaker, "The canal gates are seven feet thick and range from 47 to 82 feet high depending on their position. They must hold back a considerable weight of water and be strong enough to withstand accidents. A failure at the gate could unleash a flood of water downstream. The gates can only be opened when the water level on both sides is equal."

Faith continued, "Each lock chamber holds 26,700,000 U.S. gallons of water. The Pegasus is about to enter the first of three locks. When it's in the first chamber, the water level will rise to bring it to the next level. In total, the ship must rise 85 feet to get to Gatun Lake. If the ship was transiting all the way to the Pacific Ocean, it would need to be lowered 85 feet down and traverse three locks—the single step Pedro Miguel and the two-step Miraflores."

Marshall got very excited while explaining to Alec how the gate operating machinery worked. It was obvious that Weissman had learned about the canal's intricacies prior to taking the cruise. Most of it went over Alec's head and the others had their eyes fixed upon the thin piece of land that separated the two lanes of ship's traffic entering and leaving the canal.

The cruise director's disembodied voice pointed out, "Ships are guided through the lock chambers by electric locomotives, known as *mulas* or mules. The mules run on paired five-foot broad gauge railway tracks and are attached to the ship with strong cables. They keep the ship centered in the canal and help control braking. Forward motion into and through the chamber is provided by the ship's engines."

When the Pegasus pulled up to the gates of the second chamber, Marshall excused himself to go to the aft section of the ship to watch the rear gates close behind him. Alec watched as he nearly ran over an elderly passenger entering the bow."

Annette shook her head in dismay while Michael commented, "He's like a hyped-up kid in a candy store today."

Jen added, "I think he's sweet."

Her remark prompted Alec to think of the Panama buns that Paige wanted for breakfast. As the threesome watched the water level rise, along with the ship, Alec collected four of the pastries.

Before leaving the two women, Alec said, "I may see you later. Paige and I are going to take the 'Shaping of Panama' excursion when the ship finishes its transit to Gatun Lake."

Jen Bristow gushed in response, "Michael and I have reserved that one, too. And, if I'm not mistaken, I believe your captain and Emily also booked it. I think they make a handsome couple."

Though Alec wanted to observe the captain with Ms. Irving, he was less than eager to have Charles Stewart on his tour. Hoping that the cruise line had arranged for several coaches to take passengers to Panama City, Alec set off for his suite.

Alec entered the cabin and sniffed the air. It was fragrant with the odor of freshly brewed coffee. Alec didn't know what excited him more—Paige still wearing her silky nightgown, or his oversized coffee mug filled with the magical elixir.

After enjoying their breakfast, Alec checked his watch and suggested, "We'd better get ready for our daytrip."

Paige agreed, "Go ahead, shave and shower. I need to pack my tote with some essentials like bug spray and sunscreen. I understand it's going to be in the mid-nineties today, and I don't want either of us to get sunstroke."

Alec disappeared into the bathroom and when he emerged, the bed was made and on the covers was a pair of tan shorts and a button-down Hawaiian shirt. Next to them was a floral sundress and large brimmed straw hat.

While Paige hurried into the vacated room to shower, Alec called, "I guess the shorts are for me."

Alec heard Paige laugh and retort, "I think the captain might object to seeing you in my dress." Any other remarks were drowned out by running water.

Thirty minutes later, the DunBartons were ready. Since the ship was just transiting out of the third lock, Alec and Paige headed to the Lido Deck to get a birds eye view of the canal and pick up snacks for their upcoming trip.

At the Lido Buffet, Alec filled empty sandwich baggies with pieces of fruit, slices of cheese, and assorted rolls. He added it to Paige's already bulging tote bag. Paige then decided to peruse some Panama Canal souvenirs that were being sold poolside. She stopped in front of a table selling men's straw hats.

After placing one on Alec's head, she pronounced, "It makes you look dashing and more handsome than ever. Alec let Paige purchase it for him. Even though it wasn't an authentic Panamanian hat, Alec agreed it would protect him from the damaging rays of the sun.

The group tours were called minutes later. A voice on the loudspeaker instructed guests who had purchased excursions to go to the Starlight Lounge to collect their colored and numbered tour stickers. With a few others, Alec and Paige headed to the elevator.

The DunBartons took seats in the lower level of the lounge and awaited further instructions. A member of the excursion team was on hand and told a few groups to head down to the Main Deck. When he announced, "Group, Red One, the 'Shaping of Panama,'" several people in the audience rose. Among them were Emily Irving and Captain Stewart. Charles looked like a typical tourist wearing a real Panama hat on his bald head.

Alec cautioned Paige to walk behind them when they were directed to a small boat tied up to the port side of the ship. The ride to Gatun Lake's shore took just minutes. From Alec's vantage point, he could see Stewart animatedly talking to Emily. It jarred Alec. The captain always appeared so reserved on the ship.

The passengers were then directed to take seats on the bus parked near the dock. Alec wanted Paige to sit near them but far enough away to remain unobserved. Alec's plans were thwarted when the captain called, "I saw you earlier. There are empty seats in front of us. Take them. Over the ninety-minute ride to Panama City, I'm sure we'll have something to say to each other."

Once seated, Paige turned to Alec and winked.

The coach filled up quickly. Although Jen Bristow and Michael Donovan were not on their bus, Alec didn't mind. With the captain and Emily sitting behind him, he assumed he'd have his hands full.

When everyone was on board, a middle-aged man, dressed rather dapperly, stood up in front of the passengers. His voice was well-modulated, and he introduced himself as Alonzo. He clearly explained, "You're on the 'Shaping of Panama' excursion. Over the next ninety minutes, I'm going to tell you about Panama, the original canal, and its later expansion. Please sit back and relax."

The bus started and after making several turns, the tour guide stated, "We're now traveling on the Atlantic Bridge that your ship passed under a few hours ago. A distance of fifty miles separates the Port of Colon and Panama City. We will be taking the Trans-Isthmus Highway to the Pacific Ocean. The route roughly parallels the canal's waterway."

He then took a moment to hand out a map to the coach's passengers. Alec and Paige took one eagerly. Though they had traversed the Panama Canal many times in the last few months, Alec was glad to have a copy and began to study it.

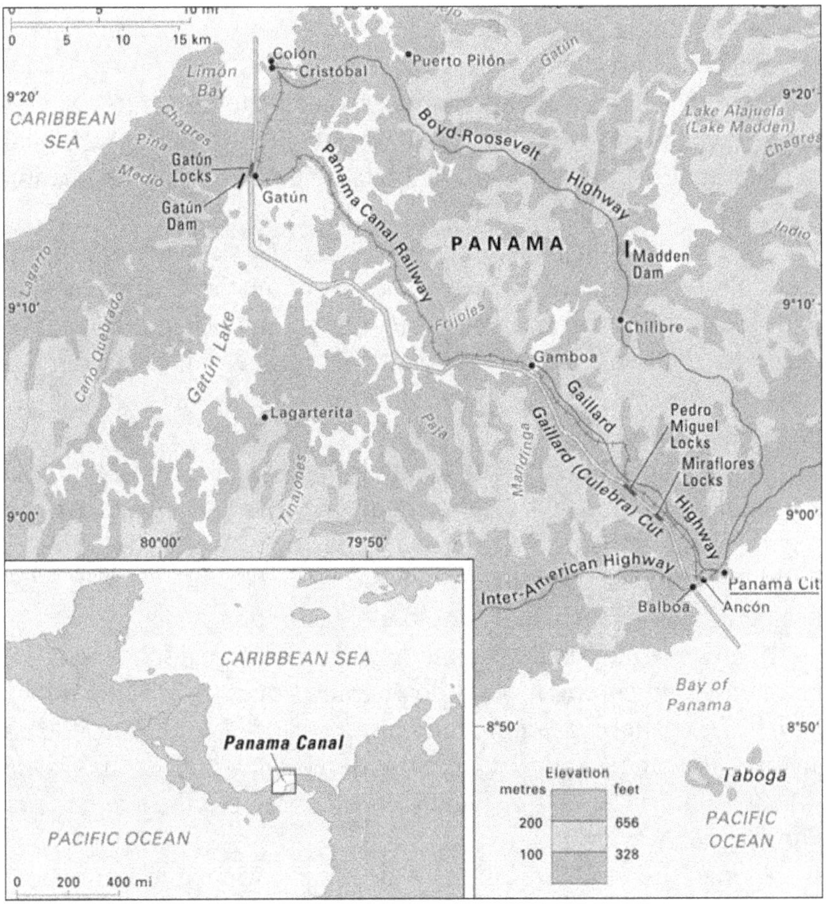

When everyone had a copy, Alonzo continued, "I've given you a map of the original Panama Canal. The French tried to build a sea-level canal in 1881. Unlike the government's success in constructing the Suez Canal on flat, desert terrain, French builders in Panama had difficulty in excavating land in the thick jungles.

They lost nearly twenty thousand laborers from accidents and tropical diseases, such as yellow fever and malaria.

"French hospital workers also believed that malaria was 'mala aira' or bad air and set out pots of flowers in still water. Instead of eradicating mosquitoes, the real cause of malaria, they made circumstances worse.

"In 1889, France abandoned the project, and the Unites States, under President McKinnley, toyed with the idea of building a canal in Nicaragua. That plan was eventually rejected because the nation was prone to earthquakes."

Alec noted that Nicaragua was above Costa Rica and not a particularly good site for a route connecting the Caribbean Sea with the Pacific Ocean. Even though the country had a large lake close to the west coast, builders would have had to dig up considerably more land. Upon pointing out Lake Nicaragua on the map, Paige agreed.

Alonzo continued, "The United States took control of the Panama Canal in 1904. The first task of the Americans was to upgrade infrastructure, improve sanitation, renovate French buildings, recruit laborers, and build new housing. It was also decided that the new canal should include a lock system.

"The Panama Canal officially opened on August 15, 1914. The planned grand ceremony was downgraded due to the outbreak of WWI. The canal was completed at a cost of 375 million dollars and was the most expensive construction project in U.S. history up to that point. In 1999, President Carter transferred the canal to the Panamanian government."

Alonzo then took questions. One person wanted to know how much it cost for a ship the size of the Pegasus to transit the waterway. When he announced the amount. Alec looked behind him to see Captain Stewart's expression. He responded with a solemn nod and Alec wondered whether the ship got a discount since it wasn't going through the entire canal.

Another person wanted to know about the Panama Canal Extension project, which allowed large ships known as New or Neo-Panamax to travel from coast to coast.

Alonzo apologized and said, "I don't have a map to give out, but its three new locks were excavated a short distance east of the Gatun Locks, and the three Pacific locks to the southwest of the Miraflores Locks. All the ships use the same passageway.

"The chambers of the Neo-Panamax Locks are much larger than the originals and can accommodate vessels 1,400 feet long, 180 feet wide, and 60 feet deep. The old locks only allowed ships 1,000 feet long, 110 feet wide, and 41 feet deep to fit comfortably. That project ran from 2007 to 2016."

When the bus drew closer to Panama City, Alonzo started to point out places of interest. The scenery had changed dramatically from a rural area to a metropolis filled with sparkling high-rise apartments and businesses. The number of towering glass and metallic buildings was staggering.

Before Alec could stop himself, he sang out,

Jump back, what's that sound?
Here she comes, full blast and top down
Hot shoe, burnin' down the avenue
Model citizen, zero discipline
Don't you know she's coming home with me
You'll lose her in the turn
I'll get her

Panama, Panama
Panama, Panama

Ain't nothin' like it, her shiny machine
Got the feel for the wheel, keep the moving parts clean
Hot shoe, burnin' down the avenue
Got an on ramp comin' through my bedroom
Don't you know she's coming home with me
You'll lose her in the turn
I'll get her

Panama, Panama
Panama, Panama

Yeah, we're runnin' a little bit hot tonight

I can barely see the road from the heat comin' off of it
Ah, you reach down, between my legs and ease the seat back
She's blinding, I'm flying
Right behind the rear-view mirror now
Got the feeling, power steering
Pistons popping, ain't no stopping now

Panama, Panama
Panama, Panama
Panama, Panama
Panama

Paige and Alec turned around to see whether Captain Stewart heard him. Instead of receiving an indifferent stare, the captain corrected, "That song by Van Halen is about a car, not a country."

Alec didn't know how to react and then laughed, "I think I need to change my original opinion of you, Sir." In response, the captain flashed him a tolerant smile.

The coach continued through the city. Between tall buildings, Alec and Paige caught sight of the Pacific Ocean. When they traversed a road that was surrounded by water on both sides, Alonzo announced, "We're on the Amador Causeway. It was constructed with rock that was excavated from the Panama Canal. It connects the mainland with four small islands. On Flamenco Island, we'll be having a buffet lunch at Bucanero's Restaurant."

Gazing at the lovely blue waters, Paige exclaimed, "It's hard to believe that my family lives off the same Pacific Ocean. I feel closer to them here even though they're over four thousand miles away!"

Alec nodded but replied, "We're actually closer to them when we're in Fort Lauderdale. Our home port is just three thousand miles from San Francisco." Noting her glum expression, Alec added, "On our next vacation, we'll definitely visit your relatives in California."

Paige smiled, "Yes, we must. We still need to make the acquaintance of my nephew. He's about six weeks old now."

Moments later, the bus came to a stop and parked near the informal restaurant. While getting off the coach, Alec pointed out the palm trees surrounding the eatery. It was obvious from the white sand beach, cute shops, and private fishing boats that the area attracted tourists from all over.

The restaurant had a large bar and was adorned inside and out with pirate décor. The wooden beams on the slanted ceiling added to the rustic tone. The sightseers were told to take a seat at any vacant table, give the servers their beverage order, and get in line for the buffet.

Paige took a table near the food station. Since their table sat four and the captain and Emily were right behind him, Alec turned around and invited, "Would you like to share this table?"

Alec watched Stewart's face. It looked like he was weighing the options—sit with employees or two of the ship's passengers. He ended up thanking Alec and pulled out a chair for Emily.

While the men ordered beers all around, the ladies visited the restroom. When they returned, everyone went up to the buffet. Alec lined up first and announced, "There's crusty bread, butter, salad, mixed vegetables, mashed potatoes, chicken breast with peppers, and some sort of beef thing."

Paige turned to Emily and whispered, "My husband is a foody and loves to eat."

Emily smiled, "I'm glad nothing appears too highly seasoned. I wonder if they serve different meals to the locals."

When the captain saw how much food Alec had on his plate, he quipped, "Now, I understand why the ship's grocery bills are so high."

Alec took it good naturedly and led the way back to their table. Over lunch, the foursome discussed the trip so far. They all thought that Alonzo was well informed and had made the long drive feel much shorter.

Stewart shared, "This is my first outing since I arrived on the Pegasus, and I must say, I'm impressed. I have to hand it to my excursion team."

Emily agreed, "I've taken several tours, and they've all been wonderful. Tomorrow, I'm going on a jungle cruise in Costa Rica."

The captain gazed at Emily warmly. "I wish I could join you. Unfortunately, the ship requires my attention."

Emily crinkled her nose in affection and patted Stewart's arm. "I am so happy you were able to accompany me on this excursion."

Alec engaged Paige in some quiet conversation hoping that his two suspects would not notice they were being watched. Alec really didn't think that the captain had murdered Aaron Sloane but was not as sure about Emily. The biblical archeologist had made it no secret that she loathed Sloane.

The meal ended all too soon. After everyone was served flan for dessert, Alonzo announced that they should get ready to reboard the bus.

On the way to the coach, Emily winked at Charles Stewart and said, "I bet you'd make a realistic swashbuckling captain."

He responded dryly, "You mean, I'm not now?"

CHAPTER TWELVE

▼

"Live to Tell"
Words & Music by Madonna Ciccone and Pat Leonard
Genre: Pop Rock, Released: March 1986

Sunday Afternoon—11th of February

After lunch, the bus headed to Old Panama or *Panamá Viejo*. While traveling through the streets, Alonzo explained, "Old Panama was founded in 1519 and became the first permanent European settlement on the Pacific Ocean. Upon its creation, the city became an important base where gold and silver was collected and sent to Spain.

"The town grew to 10,000 inhabitants in 1670. On January 28, 1671, the Welsh privateer, Henry Morgan, and his men attacked the city. They marched from the Caribbean coast and across the jungle. Morgan's force defeated the town's militia and proceeded to sack Panama. A fire, either started by Morgan or an accidental explosion of the gunpowder magazines caused the old city to burn. The attack caused the loss of thousands of lives and the new city of Panama had to be rebuilt a few kilometers to the west of the old site."

Though Alonzo's remarks were interesting, it was difficult to imagine what the town had looked like. The only historic sites that could be viewed from the bus were the ruins of a church, a convent, and some military buildings.

From that location, the coach took them to *Casco Viejo* or the Spanish Quarter. It was settled in 1673 after the near-total destruction of Old Panama City. The new town was built on a peninsula, completely surrounded by the sea and a defensive system of walls. In 1997, it was designated a World Heritage Site.

The bus stopped on a side street where the passengers were told to disembark. Alec and Paige were glad to stretch their legs and go on the walking tour. As the group followed Alonzo, it became obvious that through gentrification, the area had become a tourist hotspot filled with restaurants, boutique hotels, and nightclubs. There were also many churches, museums, and historic homes to explore.

The DunBartons got to appreciate the architecture in the quaint city squares, which blended French, Spanish, and Italian styles. Paige especially liked the black wrought iron second and third-story balconies that adorned the yellow, pink, and white residences.

Although Alec enjoyed the walk, he found the heat became intolerable at times. The sun was unrelenting and while following Alonzo, Alec tried to stay on the shady side of the street. When the group finally entered an ornate church, Alec happily sat down on a pew and took photos of the stained-glass windows from afar.

Paige admitted to feeling exhausted, too. She seemed to come back to life when the tour guide directed them to a shopping area. Before letting his charges spend their money, Alonzo warned, "If you're going to buy a real Panamanian hat, make sure it's from Ecuador. We don't make them here. Authentic hats usually cost forty dollars or more."

On the way back to the bus, the group also stopped by a street market that contained, colorful woven handbags, children's toys made out of wood, beaded jewelry, and straw hats. After being given a half hour to shop at that locale, they were directed to a lookout point where the air-conditioned coach was waiting for them.

During the walking tour, Alec had lost track of Stewart and Emily. He was relieved to see them bring up the rear, behind several tired stragglers. When the captain approached Alec's aisle in the bus, he proposed, "Let's sit together on the ride back to Colon. It will give me a chance to hear how your investigation is going."

Paige smiled as she gave Captain Stewart her seat. Upon getting in beside Emily, the women immediately began talking about their purchases. Alec gave up on trying to eavesdrop, certain that Paige would give him a complete report later in the evening.

On the drive back to Colon, Alec got to know the captain better. Although it was difficult to break through the captain's reserve, he learned that Charles Stewart was not humorless. At times, his witticisms concerning the ship and the crew were exactly on target. Alec would have liked him to continue in that vein.

Unfortunately, Stewart got to the point about twenty minutes later and demanded, "Where are you on your investigation? Are you any closer to naming the person who poisoned Aaron Sloane with fentanyl?"

With a solemn air, Alec replied, "I've been in touch with my contact at the Fort Lauderdale Homicide Department and have learned that the fentanyl in the nasal spray contained impurities and had probably been purchased on the street. He's looking into the FAO members to see if any of them had a drug problem. Since the drug is so plentiful, it's unlikely he'll be able to find the source."

Stewart grunted, "I see."

"It also appears," Alec resumed, "one of the FAO members sailing with us was named in Sloane's last will and testament and in line to receive half of his large estate. Alec didn't want to say any more about the subject since Charles was not an impartial observer.

Therefore, Alec was stunned when the captain remarked, "I understand that Sloane believed Jen Bristow was his daughter."

Alec's jaw dropped open in response and managed to say, "How did you know?"

Stewart's facial expression softened as he uttered, "Emily is very observant and had noted on several occasions that Sloane treated Miss Bristow like a beloved child."

Alec nodded, wondering what else Emily may have noticed. The two men continued to talk until they reached the port in Colon. From the window, Alec could see that the town was nothing like Panama City. Instead of sparkling new skyscrapers, the area looked rundown with ramshackle buildings and graffiti covered warehouses.

The bus stopped soon after in front of the terminal building. The sun was setting behind the passengers as they disembarked the coach. While letting the ladies go ahead, the captain warned Alec, "Keep me apprised of the situation."

Paige waited for Alec at the curb. Upon handing the bus driver and tour guide a nice tip for their safe and informative excursion, Alec whispered to Paige, "Did you learn anything from Emily?"

Winking, Paige affirmed, "I did. But I'm exhausted and need to wash up. Let's go back to the cabin. While I take my bath, you can rustle up dinner. After that, I promise to tell you everything."

Though Alec was eager to hear about Emily, Alec did as he was told. From his suite, he took the elevator up to the Lido Deck to pick up two meals. Paige just wanted something light and requested a mixed salad. Alec, on the other hand, was hungry and stopped by the carvery for slices of leg of lamb, roasted potatoes, grilled squash, and mint sauce.

On his return to the cabin, Alec placed the heavy tray of food on the kitchenette's counter and walked over to the bathroom. Paige was still luxuriating in the bubbly tub with her head resting on a rolled-up towel. Her eyes were closed and when she opened them, she smiled, "I see you're back already. Would you mind if I soak another ten minutes?"

Alec took a seat on the edge of the tub and replied, "I might be persuaded, if you tell me what Emily had to say."

With a relaxed sigh, Paige began. "Emily and I got to talking about our families. I mentioned that my brother Derek and his wife

Gail just had a baby boy, and I was anxious to see them. While I was showing her pictures of Oliver, she reacted oddly."

"What did she do?" Alec urged.

Gazing at Alec, Paige replied, "Emily shuddered and said, 'Poor Lena died before she could look into the eyes of her newborn.'"

Alec questioned, "She was pregnant when she died?"

"Apparently," Paige answered. "Lena would have been pregnant five or six months when she passed away. Emily spoke to her a few days before she left for Panama. Lena told her that she believed in God and miracles again. Emily was thrilled for her and wished her well. She didn't know then that Lena was planning to divorce Aaron or that someone else could be the baby's father."

With conflicting thoughts going through his mind. Alec sang,

I have a tale to tell
Sometimes, it gets so hard to hide it well
I was not ready for the fall
Too blind to see the writing on the wall

A man can tell a thousand lies
I've learned my lesson well
Hope I live to tell the secret I have learned
'Til then, it will burn inside of me

I know where beauty lives
I've seen it once. I know the warmth she gives
The light that you could never see
It shines inside, you can't take that from me

A man can tell a thousand lies
I've learned my lesson well
Hope I live to tell the secret I have learned
'Til then, it will burn inside of me

The truth is never far behind
You kept it hidden well
If I live to tell the secret I knew
Then will I ever have the chance again?

If I ran away, I'd never have the strength to go very far
How would they hear the beating of my heart?
Will it grow cold, the secret that I hide? Will I grow old?
How will they hear? When will they learn? How will they know?

A man can tell a thousand lies
I've learned my lesson well
Hope I live to tell the secret I have learned
'Til then, it will burn inside of me

The truth is never far behind
You kept it hidden well
If I live to tell the secret I knew
Then will I ever have the chance again?

A man can tell a thousand lies
I've learned my lesson well
Hope I live to tell the secret I have learned
'Til then, it will burn inside of me

Paige complimented Alec on his rendition of the Madonna song and remarked, "It's very apt. I wonder who the expectant father was."

Alec agreed, "I wonder," as he watched Paige rise from the bath and wrap a terrycloth robe around her wet body. For a moment, all thoughts of Lena disappeared from Alec's mind.

Paige quickly reminded Alec that his hot meal was getting cold. While they had their supper, the pair discussed Captain Stewart and Emily Irving. Both felt that their relationship had moved from fondness to intimacy.

Alec had seen Charles place his hand on Emily's hip and their glances expressed more than friendship. Though it seemed unlikely that Emily killed Sloane, Alec wasn't ready to take her off his list of suspects. Sloane considered himself a catch and did not take his marriage vows seriously. It was possible that he once tried to seduce Emily or worse.

After cleaning up the kitchenette, Paige moved to the bedroom to relax and finish a book she had started reading days earlier. It gave Alec an opportunity to send an email to Dan McGill on his laptop. In minutes, he had his computer open and wrote:

Subj: Need more information
Date: 11th of February, 8:28:01 PM EST
From: AlecDunBarton@aol.com
To: Dan.McGill@coflso.net

Dan,

It has come to my attention that Lena Sloane may have been five to six months pregnant when she died. Is it possible for you to get the autopsy results from your source in Panama? I feel this case hinges on Lena and her activities before she died.

I've learned that Victor Bristow and Marshall Weissman both had affairs with Lena Sloane and could have been the expectant father of her child. Victor was also aware that his wife, Laura, had a short affair with Aaron years ago. After confessing to it, she made her husband take a DNA test. It confirmed that Jennifer is Victor's biological daughter. I've yet to speak to Jen to find out what family secrets she may have tried to conceal.

I wish I had more to go on. The cruise will be ending in three days and, if something doesn't break soon, you might have to take over from me when the ship docks in Fort Lauderdale this Thursday. In the meantime, have you learned whether any the FAO members or their relatives have been arrested for drug use?

If you discover anything more, please let me know right away.

Regards,
Alec

Alec sent the message feeling that time was closing in on him. After putting away his laptop, Alec got ready for bed. Paige had just closed her book with a satisfied smile.

Noting Alec's demeanor, Paige urged, "Don't worry yet. You're going on the same excursion as Annette Perkins and Marshall Weissman tomorrow."

Alec's pained expression turned hopeful as he got into bed. Since the Tortuguero tour in Costa Rica wasn't scheduled to leave until twelve thirty, he'd have plenty of time to track down Jen and Victor in the morning.

Upon giving Paige a goodnight kiss and turning off the light, Alec turned onto his side. Even though the soft sound of Paige breathing was soothing, sleep eluded him for several hours.

CHAPTER THIRTEEN

"Bungle in the Jungle"
Words & Music by Ian Anderson
Genre: Progressive Rock, Released: October 1974

**Monday Morning—12th of February**

Despite having six hours of sleep, Alec woke up refreshed. It was nine o'clock. After propping up his pillows, he reached for his mug that was sitting on the bedside table. As usual, Paige had thoughtfully left him a cup of coffee and a snack to go with it. He was halfway through his small breakfast when he realized he'd better get going.

He had waited long enough for Victor to speak to Jen about his past indiscretion with Lena and his wife's affair with Aaron Sloane. Alec downed the rest of his coffee in one gulp and brushed the chocolate chip cookie crumbs off the covers.

In twenty minutes, Alec managed to shower, shave, and dress. His first job was to locate Miss Bristow.

Alec found the young woman on the Lido Deck, sitting at a table by the pool with Michael Donovan. She was wearing sunglasses and a large, brimmed straw hat. Alec wondered whether she had overindulged the night before or was just trying to look mysterious.

Upon getting closer, Alec could see that she looked miserable and asked whether he could join them, Protectively, Michael said, "Now, is not a great time."

Undaunted, Alec pulled out the spare chair and asked Jen, "You spoke to your father?"

Taking off her glasses with one quick movement, she snarled, "You ruined my life! You dug up secrets that should have stayed hidden. Does everyone know about my family? Who have you told!"

Alec felt sorry for Jen Bristow and immediately tried to allay her fears. Quietly, Alec promised, "No one knows and none of it will come out as long as you, your dad, or mother didn't kill Aaron Sloane."

Michael spoke up. "Jen's mother couldn't have had anything to do with it. She's been crippled with arthritis for years and hardly leaves the house."

Alec argued, "It's possible she doctored Sloane's nasal spray before he came on this cruise. She didn't have to be on this trip to kill him."

"That's ridiculous!" Jen cried. "What proof do you have?"

Realizing he was bungling his interview with Jen, Alec took a different tack and explained, "I really don't think your mother was involved. I was merely trying to keep my options open. I need to know how you reacted when you learned that Aaron Sloane left you 50% of his estate."

In response, Jen turned to Michael with wide eyes and an open mouth. Alec had a hard time imagining that the young woman was feigning surprise.

"Didn't your father tell you?" Alec demanded.

Jen shook her head with a dumfounded expression. "Dad told me that Sloane thought he was my father because he once had an affair with my mom. But to leave me money? I can't believe it! I just considered Aaron a creepy friend of my parents."

Alec's attention turned to Donovan and said, "You've worked for Sloane and must have been privy to conversations between your boss and other employees. Did you have any inkling that Jen was to inherit?"

Once again, Donovan reacted like a boy scout. Michael's blue eyes locked onto Alec's brown ones with complete innocence. Alec found himself gazing at Donovan's hands to see if he was holding up three fingers in the famous scout salute.

Michael responded, "You have to believe me. Sloane was always careful to keep his personal and business affairs private. When Marshall and I were on *The Sultry Siren,* we stayed in crew quarters, a distance away from Sloane's office and his quarters."

Alec had to take his word for it, having no proof that he was lying. For several minutes, the threesome conversed about the probate process and Jen's inheritance. What had started out as an angry confrontation had turned into a civilized conversation.

When Alec asked her where he might find her dad, she suggested the Holmes Media Center. Ready for a snack from the library's café, Alec departed. He needed to have a brief word with Victor to confirm that Jen had told him the truth.

On seeing Victor Bristow seated at a brown leather recliner in the media center, Alec stopped by the café to pick up a second cup of coffee with a brioche bun filled with ham, cheese, and pickle relish. After satisfying his hunger, Alec carried his nearly empty cup of coffee to Victor and pulled up a spare club chair.

Not hiding his feelings, Victor sneered, "You again!"

Alec gave him a halfhearted smile and apologized, "I'm sorry you had to bare your soul to your daughter but lies and falsehoods have a way of bubbling up to the surface. I just spoke to Jen, and I think she has accepted everything you told her."

Victor put down the crossword puzzle he was working on and gazed at Alec. 'I'm glad she's settled down. Last night, I told her about my affair with Lena and her mother's short dalliance with Sloane. She said she couldn't stand to be with me and left to go drinking with Michael. I'm not sure what upset me more, having her angry at me or spending the night drinking."

Alec let Victor express his thoughts and then asked, "Why didn't you tell Jennifer about the inheritance?"

Victor shook his head. "I had no time. She dashed out of my cabin like it was on fire. How did she react when you told her?"

Alec suspected that Victor was being truthful and replied, "Pretty well." Alec didn't bother to add almost *too* well.

From the Holmes Media Center, Alec stopped by his office to see how Regina was doing and to check his email for a reply from Dan McGill. Before signing onto his computer, he brought Regina up to date on his investigation. When all her questions were answered, Alec clicked open his inbox.

Thrilled to see a message from the detective, he read:

Subj: More Info
Date: 12th of February, 10:05:51 AM EST
From: Dan.McGill@coflso.net
To: AlecDunBarton@aol.com

Alec,

This morning, my contact in Panama faxed me Lena Sloane's autopsy results. A terciopelo (fer-de-lance) snake bit her on the ankle. The snake is highly venomous, and the toxin destroyed the flesh around the site. As the poison traveled through her body, it caused internal bleeding and organ failure. Blood had seeped through her nose, lips, and gums. Ninety percent of victims bitten by the fer-de-lance die.

Lena Sloane had to be carried by two male college students from her location to the campsite where the snake bite kit was stored. The kit only contained a venom suction extractor, which was useless since the flesh around the site had swollen.

The report stated that Aaron Sloane took his wife to the closest emergency room, minutes away. The Sub Centro de Salud El Caño Hospital didn't have the facilities or the antivenom to treat Lena and had to transfer her to a medical center in Panama City. It took some time for her to get the right antivenom and the doctors were unable to save her.

As you know, the Panamanian police investigated Aaron Sloane, suspecting that he delayed getting his wife medical treatment. It now seems that the time taken for hospital staff to transfer Lena from El Caño to Panama City also contributed to her death. More importantly, I can confirm that Lena Sloane was nearly six months pregnant when she died.

I hope this helps,
Dan

Alec must have exclaimed out loud and Regina rose from her desk to ask, "What happened? What did McGill say?"

Alec relayed, "Lena was six months pregnant when she died. When do women begin to show? Aaron must have noticed and wondered whether the baby was his. Why did she even go to Panama under those circumstances?"

Regina answered Alec's first question and replied, "Slender and very heavy women can often hide their condition for many months. It also depends on what clothes a woman usually wears and if it's her first pregnancy."

Pausing a moment, she added, "It would be much easier to tell if she was naked."

Alec agreed with that. As to his other questions, Alec returned to McGill's email and requested the homicide detective to locate one or more of the college students who went on the dig and find out:

1. Was Lena Sloane visibly pregnant?
2. Did she argue with Aaron over her condition?
3. What motivated Lena to go on that dig while pregnant?
4. What did the film crew know about Sloane's relationship with his wife?

After pressing the send icon, Alec glanced at his watch and saw it was 11:15 AM. Realizing that he was supposed to meet his tour group on the pier at noon, he said a hurried goodbye to Regina and rushed to his cabin to change into shorts and pick up his straw hat, bug spray, and sunscreen.

With his pockets bulging, Alec disembarked the ship and headed over to an outdoor market, near the bus excursion area, to wait in the shade. The shops were selling a great multitude of items that included Costa Rican tee shirts, tote bags, hats, jewelry, and handmade toys.

Alec noticed Annette Perkins at one of the stalls fingering a colorful sundress that appeared far too small for her boxy body. Although the vendor lowered his price twice, she sadly shook her head and continued down the row.

After purchasing a small bag of Costa Rican coffee from another stall, Annette noticed Alec. With an almost shy smile, she approached him and asked, "Are you going on an excursion? Most of them left very early this morning. I couldn't face waking up at dawn two days in a row."

Glad she looked less like a bull dog and more like a smiling Bichon Frisé, Alec greeted, "I'm taking the Tortuguero Canal jungle pontoon boat ride. Though he knew she had booked the same one, he asked, "Which are you going on?"

Perkins replied, "I'm going on that one also. I understand we'll be seeing orchids, water lilies, tropical birds, monkeys, crocodiles, sloths, and toucans. I just hope it won't be buggy."

Alec smiled, "We can share my insect repellent."

Annette seemed to blush from his remark and again, Alec wondered what had gotten into the standoffish president. His musings came to an end when she pointed to a young woman with a sign and said, "I think she's the tour guide for our excursion. We'd better line up by her coach."

Alec followed Perkins. While waiting to board the bus, Marshall drew up to them, out of breath, sunburned, and perspiring. He managed to say, "It's going to be another hot day. I hope the boat has a canopy or some sort of covering."

Annette gazed at the tech nerd with disgust while he wiped his brow with the back of his hand. Alec hadn't noticed earlier that the two archaeologists were less than cordial to each other.

The awkwardness ended when the tour guide began to check off the names of those waiting from a list on a clipboard. After noting that she was missing two people, she announced to the group, "My name is Anahi, and I will be your tour guide to the Tortuguero Canal ecological boat ride. You can board the coach while we wait for additional passengers."

Alec wasn't sure who to sit with. He gave Annette his arm to help her mount the first rung of the bus. Once aboard, she beckoned him and patted the empty seat beside her. Marshall was right behind him and took a vacant spot on the aisle.

This was the first time that Alec could recall a suspect in a murder case wanting his attention. Hoping to find out the reason for Annette's sudden friendliness, Alec sat down with a smile.

The last two passengers arrived five minutes later and grabbed the remaining seats in the back of the bus. Anahi then introduced herself again along with Luis, the bus driver. During the short drive to the park, the tour guide told the group about the country's weather, history, economy, and people.

When there was a pause in her speech, Alec turned to Annette and asked, "Did you ever meet Lena Sloane?"

Annette touched Alec's hand as she responded, "I got to know her when Aaron was president of the FAO. He served two four-year terms as president and had less than pleasant things to say about my leadership."

Alec nodded and tried to get her back on the subject of Lena by asking again, "What did you think of Mrs. Sloane?"

"She was," Annette began. "How can I say it without sounding spiteful?" Undeterred, she continued, "Lena was a woman that knew what she wanted and didn't let anything stop her from getting it. Often it was men. At other times, it was an archaeological project or a prime dig site for her TV mini-series. As you may or may not know, Lena was extremely photogenic."

Annette added grudgingly, "She had a way of making archaeology fascinating to the general public."

Alec was finally getting a picture of Aaron Sloane's deceased wife. Deciding to thoroughly research her on the internet, Alec asked Annette, "Did you know she was pregnant when she went on her last dig in Panama?"

Perkins was surprised by Alec's question. "Her pregnant? She wasn't the type to let a baby ruin her figure. She didn't like children and barely tolerated young Jen Bristow when the families vacationed together."

Their conversation ended when the bus came to a stop in front of the tour company in Moin. The group was escorted to several waiting pontoon boats that were in the canal.

Alec had nearly forgotten that Marshall was on the excursion until the tech nerd sighed behind him, "Thank goodness those boats are shaded with a canvas covering. The air-conditioning on the bus could have been set much cooler."

Alec agreed. The air around them was hot and humid, and the lush vegetation on the river banks made conditions worse. Since Annette and others had been directed to a different pontoon, Alec welcomed Marshall and induced him to share his bench on the open-air boat. Weissman looked miserable as he swatted away an insect.

A fellow wearing an orange shirt and black slacks came onboard and greeted everyone, After handing out bottles of cold water and bananas, he used the microphone to go over safety rules. Alec laughed speculating whether any passenger was crazy enough to jump out of the boat or put his or her hands in the crocodile-invested water.

The twin motors started shortly later and as the pontoon picked up speed on the twisty canal, Alec felt a welcome breeze. Marshall appeared to relax too and swallowed half his water in one gulp.

The tour guide, Miguel, explained, "Tortuguero Canals are the second largest wetland in my country and is considered to be the Amazon of Costa Rica for its natural richness and biodiversity. As we travel along the canal, I will let you know when I spot wildlife.

"Please tell me if you see something that I've missed. I'll stop the engines for you to take photographs. If you're unable to see from your seat, feel free to come up to the bow when the boat stops."

With that said, Alec looked at the dark, opaque waters for movement. Seconds later, Miquel instructed the passengers to look to their left to see a monkey in a tree and to their right to view a sleeping crocodile on a muddy bank.

Unable to contain himself, Alec sang out,

Walking through forests of palm tree apartments
Scoff at the monkeys who live in their dark tents
Down by the waterhole, drunk every Friday
Eating their nuts, saving their raisins for Sunday
Lions and tigers who wait in the shadows
They're fast but they're lazy, and sleep in green meadows

Well, let's bungle in the jungle
Well, that's all right by me, yes
Well, I'm a tiger when I want love
But I'm a snake if we disagree

Just say a word and the boys will be right there
With claws at your back to send a chill through the night air
Is it so frightening to have me at your shoulder?
Thunder and lightning couldn't be bolder
I'll write on your tombstone, I thank you for dinner
This game that we animals play is a winner

Well, let's bungle in the jungle
Well, that's all right by me, yes
I'm a tiger when I want love
I'm a snake if we disagree, yes

The rivers are full of crocodile nasties
And he who made kittens put snakes in their grasp
He's a lover of life but a player of pawns
Yes, the King on his sunset lies waiting for dawn
To light up his jungle as play is resumed
The monkeys seem willing to strike up the tune

Well, let's bungle in the jungle
Well, that's all right by me, yes
I'm a tiger when I want love
And I'm a snake when we disagree, yes

> Let's bungle in the jungle
> Well, that's all right by me, yes
> Well, I'm a tiger when I want love
> I'm a snake when we disagree
>
> Well, let's bungle in the jungle
> Well, that's all right by me, yes
> I'm a tiger when I want love

Alec's voice was partially drowned out by the boat's motors. His launch into song seemed to help Marshall forget that he was hot and clammy.

For the next forty minutes, Marshall continued to talk nonstop about everything he'd seen and heard on the tour. It got to be annoying and by the time the pontoon returned to its mooring, Alec had had enough of Marshall Weissman.

The twosome ended up sitting together on the bus ride back to the ship's pier. Annette gave Alec a pitiful smile. Though Marshall had confessed to having a brief affair with Lena, Alec had trouble imaging Weissman as her lover and father of her baby. Furthermore, Alec couldn't see Marshall as a cold-blooded killer.

Deciding to put an end to his mindless prattle, Alec asked straight on, "Did you murder Aaron Sloane?"

Weissman nearly gagged. When he recovered, he looked into Alec's eyes and said, "I liked Sloane even though he often treated Lena like a possession. She was beautiful and one of the few people who respected my intelligence. I'm sorry they're both gone."

Alec followed up, "Did you know she was pregnant when she died?"

Marshall looked away and then back again. With a tear in his eye, he replied, "I did. She had hoped it was mine!"

Recalling the Jethro Tull lyrics, Alec pondered whether Marshall was a tiger when he made love and a snake when he was angry.

CHAPTER FOURTEEN

▼

"Honesty"
Words & Music by Billy Joel
Genre: Soft Rock, Released: May 1979

Monday Afternoon—12th of February

Upon returning to the ship, Alec stopped by his cabin to freshen up. As he was about to take off again, his cell phone vibrated in his pocket. Since he rarely got personal phone calls while at sea, Alec nearly swiped the red icon on the screen before noting that the caller was Dan McGill.

The homicide detective asked dryly, "Did I get you at a bad time?"

Alec, grabbing a pen and a pad of paper from the kitchenette's counter, replied, "Not at all. Since you called and not emailed, can I assume you found out something that has a bearing on my case?"

McGill chuckled, "I may have just wanted to hear your Scottish accent."

"Ahh, how sweet," Alec replied. Becoming more serious, he asked, "What have you learned?"

While McGill talked, Alec jotted down the names of three college students who went on the dig in Panama. Though the names meant nothing to him, Alec gasped when McGill announced, "The forth student was Jennifer Bristow."

Alec was dumbfounded. During the course of his interviews with her, she had never mentioned a word to him. And, why didn't Victor say anything to him? He must have known that his daughter was with Lena on her last dig.

Now angry, he was misled by both Bristows, Alec thanked Dan for the call and made a beeline to the Churchill Room where the archaeologists had a meeting from three thirty to four thirty. Only a few of the FAO members were still in attendance when Alec arrived at 4:25 PM. None of them were among his suspects.

Curious about the dig that the Sloanes had gone on five years earlier, Alec asked the remaining archaeologists what they knew about it. One elderly woman recalled, "The Sloanes, along with several students, went to an area near El Caño Archaeological Park, southwest of Panama City. That site was first discovered in 1925 by an American adventurer while he was exploring the banks of the Panama's Rio Grande River. The fellow found ancient stone monoliths and three skeletons.

"His finds were ignored until the 1970s when a group of American archaeologists travelled to the site. They had gone to the area after learning that Spanish Conquistadors had discovered 335 pounds of golden objects buried with the people of that region."

Alec found it fascinating and urged the woman to go on."

Taking a short breath, she continued, "That group uncovered a few notable artifacts and, in the late seventies, much of Panama became off limits to foreigners. The country opened up again in the mid-1990s and, in 2005, a formal reinvestigation of El Caño was launched using new electrical surveying technology to locate the graves of pre-Columbian indigenous people.

"That team found an elite warrior dressed in a golden breastplate and adorned with jewelry made of golden beads. Since then, there have been many other important discoveries made and archaeologists believe they've hardly scratched the surface. In recent years, the site has become a tourist attraction. Visitors can take a self-guided tour of a 2011 excavation pit and see burial mounds, monoliths, and other artifacts."

Alec thanked the woman for her in-depth knowledge and was more eager than ever to locate Jennifer and Victor Bristow. From the remaining group of archaeologists, Alec learned that the FAO members had been invited to attend the Culinary Arts Center for cocktails and dinner at six thirty.

When the woman's elderly friend gushed, "The captain is hosting it," Alec realized that Stewart had recently added the event to the FAO's scheduled activities. The remaining archaeologists departed shortly later to get ready for their evening.

Not wasting a minute, Alec sought out Paige at the Future Cruise Desk. He had to wait several minutes for her to finish up with her client and then tried to sneak up behind her to land a kiss on the back of her neck.

Familiar with Alec's tactics, she swiveled her chair around just in time for him to kiss her lips. Enticed, Alec took the empty chair in front of her desk and asked, "Would you like to crash the captain's dinner party with me? If that doesn't interest you, we can go back to our cabin and have our *own* celebration."

Paige laughed, "Oh no you don't, Mister. We're going to that dinner party! Captain Stewart came by an hour ago and extended a formal invitation to us. He's going to have the quartet play dreamy music, and the chefs are going to whip up three different meals. It sounds very elegant."

Alec bowed in a stately fashion, "Your wish is my command, Lass. When is your shift over?"

Glancing at a clock on the wall of her alcove, she smiled, "I can leave now. It will give me an hour and a half to relax and get ready for the shindig."

As she took Alec's arm, Paige instructed, "You'd better wash up, too. Your skin smells like coconut sunscreen and eucalyptus bug spray."

Alec chuckled.

While Paige was soaking in the tub, Alec brought her up to date. After telling her that Jen had been one of the college students on Lena's dig, Paige questioned, "How could she have kept that from you? She knew you were interested in Lena's past. I'm afraid Ms. Bristow isn't the open book she seems."

Alec agreed and prepared to shave. As he was lathering up his cheeks and neck, Paige added, "Victor must have been aware of it as well. Not to mention, Jen's beau, Michael Donovan."

"I wouldn't be surprised if Annette also hid the truth from me," Alec groaned. Angry all over again, Alec sang out,

If you search for tenderness
It isn't hard to find
You can have the love you need to live
But if you look for truthfulness
You might just as well be blind
It always seems to be so hard to give

Honesty is such a lonely word
Everyone is so untrue
Honesty is hardly ever heard
And mostly what I need from you

I can always find someone
To say they sympathize
If I wear my heart out on my sleeve
But I don't want some pretty face
To tell me pretty lies
All I want is someone to believe

Honesty is such a lonely word
Everyone is so untrue
Honesty is hardly ever heard
And mostly what I need from you

I can find a lover
I can find a friend
I can have security
Until the bitter end
Anyone can comfort me

With promises again
I know, I know

When I'm deep inside of me
Don't be too concerned
I won't ask for nothin' while I'm gone
But when I want sincerity
Tell me where else can I turn
Cause you're the one that I depend upon

Honesty is such a lonely word
Everyone is so untrue
Honesty is hardly ever heard
And mostly what I need from you

Paige, who had risen from the tub, reached out to embrace Alec. Though she was very wet, and Alec's cheeks were still covered with shaving cream, she whispered, "I'll never lie to you!"

When Alec finally let go of his wife, her face had remnants of cream on it, and his bare chest was equally as wet as Paige's. They both laughed and Alec grumbled, "Too bad, we just have thirty minutes to get ready."

Paige winked in response and promised, "Later on tonight, we can bare our souls and other parts."

When the DunBartons arrived at the Culinary Arts Center, a sign by the door read, "Private Function." Upon entering the room, Paige and Alec looked around in awe. The lights were dimly lit, and the ship's quartet was in one corner of the lounge performing "Spring" from Vivaldi's *Four Seasons*.

On the alcove tables, which seated four to eight people, there were battery operated lights that resembled candles. Better lit were the cooking areas where baking and cooking competitions were often held. The chefs were in their makeshift kitchens and the scent of different aromas made Alec even hungrier than he had been before he entered the room.

A server, holding a tray of mixed cocktails, came up to the pair to ask which one they wanted. The young man had a gin and tonic for Paige and Alec settled for a whisky sour. Though Alec preferred single-malt Scotch whisky without ice, lemon juice, and simple syrup, he had to agree that his sour was remarkably well made and refreshing.

Another server approached with hors d'oeuvres. Alec had a hard time limiting himself to one of each variety. Annette Perkins momentarily took Alec's mind off the appetizers when she greeted the couple.

Despite the elegant setting, Alec couldn't help inquiring, "Did you know that Jennifer Bristow was one of the college students who went with the Sloanes on the El Caño dig?"

Paige eyed Alec as if to say, "Not here."

Annette's reaction was even more surprising. Nearly dropping a Swedish meatball on the floor, she moaned, "That poor girl. I knew she had gone on a few digs with her parents and the Sloanes, but I had no idea she was on *that* one." Shivering, she added, "Snakes are terrifying and to see a family friend die from a bite is really unthinkable."

Alec hadn't thought about it in that light. Jen had probably been horrified by the incident and may have tried to forget it. Temporarily cutting her some slack, Alec decided to enjoy the captain's party.

The get-together hit high gear when Charles Stewart and Emily Irving made an appearance. The captain was attired in his dress uniform, and Emily looked ethereal with her softly styled hair framing her face. She had on a lemon-yellow chiffon dress that swayed as she walked.

Alec gazed at Paige in her simple black dress and strappy sandals that accentuated her long legs. Certain he was with the most beautiful woman on the ship, Alec invited Paige to dance with him. Jen Bristow and Michael Donovan were already on the dance floor and seemed lost in each other's gazes. It didn't take long for the captain and Emily to join them.

For the remainder of the cocktail hour, the DunBartons made small talk. When the dim lights were raised, the captain welcomed the group and announced, "As an amateur archaeologist myself, I've always felt the work you professionals do is of great significance in helping people learn about their past. This is my small way of thanking you.

"You may have noticed, three of my best chefs have prepared meals for you. Please feel free to go up to each and select the entrée you want. There's beef Wellington, seafood Newburg, and a low calorie/low salt chicken dish in white wine sauce. The beverage bar is to my right and desserts to my left."

With that said, the FAO members found tables to place their unfinished cocktails and moved to the food stations. Alec and Paige waited for most of them to select their dinner before choosing something for themselves.

Alec watched them congregate into small groups. He was not surprised to see Victor, Jen, and Michael sit with Annette and Marshall. Emily took a place beside them as the captain was busy making rounds.

Since the table sat eight, Alec and Paige took the two remaining seats. Everyone appeared to be in great spirits, discussing the ambiance of the party and the flavor of the food.

Paige had chosen seafood Newburg, which was full of shrimp and scallops and coated in a sherry cream sauce. Alec was happy with his beef Wellington, green beans, and roasted potatoes. Alec wasn't surprised that Victor had selected the plain chicken dish in a wine sauce. He was a man that ate to live and not lived to eat.

Marshall ingested his dinner with gusto. While recounting the tour that Alec and he had taken on the Costa Rican canal, Alec noticed that Weissman's eyes began to glaze over. Seconds later, he started to have difficulty breathing.

When his body became limp and he dropped his fork, Alec rose from his chair and called out, "I think Mr. Weissman may be having a having a heart attack! Quick, can someone contact the infirmary?"

While Alec was loosening Marshall's tie and the top button of his shirt, the captain jumped into action. In minutes, Douglas Abbot and his team were at his side with a medical kit and wheelchair. As the doctor was examining his pupils with a penlight, he whispered to Alec, "Did you see him take any medicine or a drug?"

Alec shook his head and replied, "We both had the same meal, which he washed down with several iced teas."

Douglas continued to check him out while Paige and the captain tried to keep the onlookers at bay. Concerned that Marshall's breathing was becoming more labored, Douglas said to his aide, "Let's get him down to sickbay and place a breathing tube in his windpipe. Also, bring down his plate, beverage glass, and the iced tea urn."

Alec knew better than to question the doctor then and there. It was obvious that Douglas knew what was ailing Weissman and wanted to keep it to himself. Moments later, Marshall was whisked away leaving the FAO members to wonder what had happened to him.

Captain Stewart instructed Alec and Paige to remain behind and urged the others to finish their meals. When the musicians started to play background music again, Alec addressed the group, "Please don't worry! Marshall Weissman is in good hands, and I'm sure he'll be fine."

With that said, many of the archaeologists resumed eating and drinking. Upon retaking his seat at his table, Alec was questioned by Victor, "Do you think it was his heart?"

Alec shook his head and muttered, "I don't know."

Annette posed, "Why did the doctor want his dishes and the iced tea urn? Does he think he was poisoned?"

Alec had the same concerns and inquired, "Did Marshall take recreational drugs?"

Shyly, Jen recounted, "I saw him smoke pot a couple of times. He said it helped him relax."

In response to Alec's question regarding harder drugs, they shook their heads and said they didn't think so.

Paige wanted to know what they knew about Weissman's family and his private life.

Michael admitted, "I think he has an elderly mother with Parkinson's disease and a younger sister. I know he often wires them money to cover his mom's medical expenses. His dad died a long time ago."

Alec followed up, "Do you know anything about his health?"

Perkins replied, "He's about thirty pounds overweight, and I've seen him gobble up lots of sweets on this cruise."

Donovan agreed, "Our cabin refrigerator is full of cookies and cake. Every night, he raids the Lido Buffet for sweets and has a snack before going to bed."

Alec couldn't find fault in his behavior since he did the same thing. Paige had to periodically go through their refrigerator to get rid of half-eaten pieces of pie and cake.

While the party was winding down, Alec stopped by other tables to see how the FAO members were doing. None of them seemed too upset about Marshall's sudden illness, expecting him to make a full recovery.

When the last members of the group departed, Alec closed the door to the Culinary Arts Center and said, "Let's go down to the infirmary and see how Marshall is doing."

Paige didn't argue.

Dr. Abbot greeted the DunBartons when they entered the infirmary. He quickly dispelled their fears and reported, "Mr. Weissman is feeling better now. He was dosed with fentanyl, and I administered Naloxone via nasal spray. It took just a few minutes for his breathing to normalize."

After absorbing the information, Alec questioned, "How did you know what was wrong with him?"

The doctor grimaced, "I'm afraid I've been seeing more and more of these cases on the ship. Sometimes teenagers traveling with their elderly grandparents get into their painkillers, and I've seen older passengers overdose by accident.

"I assumed it was Marshall's issue when I saw how he was breathing and noted his constricted pupils, clammy skin, and purple lips."

Paige posed the big question and asked, "Was he poisoned or did he accidentally take too much?"

The doctor replied, "I used fentanyl strips to test the leftovers on Marshall's plate and the liquid in his beverage glass. I found fentanyl in his iced tea and none in the urn."

Alec nodded. "It looks like someone purposely laced his drink. Does fentanyl have a bitter taste? Would he have been able to detect it in sweet tea? And, was the amount high enough to kill him?"

Douglas, unable to answer the first two questions, replied to the third, "I have the poisoned iced tea from Marshall's glass. The Fort Lauderdale Police lab should be able to tell us whether it contained a deadly dose after we return to Florida."

Upon asking the doctor whether they could visit Marshall, Douglas warned Alec and Paige to keep it short. In a private room to the right of the waiting area, Weissman greeted the twosome in a jovial manner. More seriously, Marshall asked, "Do you think someone tried to kill me?"

Alec answered his question with a question and posed, "Did you have any idea what was happening to you when you started to feel ill?"

Marshall shook his head in the negative and stated, "I never use painkillers. I pride myself on my intellect, and I don't let anything interfere with the way I think or behave. I like being in control of myself and only let go the few times I smoked grass to relax."

Alec didn't think he was being deceptive and then asked, "How did you learn that your drink was laced with fentanyl?"

Marshall, making himself more comfortable in the hospital bed, replied, "Dr. Abbot told me."

Now getting to the crux of the matter, Alec followed up, "Do you know who killed Aaron Sloane? It's possible his killer sees you as a threat."

Weissman appeared surprised by that allegation and swore, "I have no idea who could have replaced Aaron's nasal spray with a toxic one. I may have been poisoned by accident. I wasn't the only one who had a glass of iced tea on the table."

Alec agreed and cast his mind back. He and Paige had water with their meal and the rest had either iced tea, lemonade, or the remainder of their cocktail. The opioid could have been meant for another person. The table was oval shaped, and their glasses were often in close proximity to each other in the center of the table."

Getting nowhere fast, Alec changed his tactics and inquired, "Did you know that Jennifer Bristow was one of the college students present on the El Caño dig with the Sloanes?"

"I hadn't when Lena died," Marshall admitted. "I learned about it a few months ago from another FAO member."

Marshall added, "I told Donovan after he started to date Jen. I don't know if she shared any of the grisly details with him. It couldn't have been very pretty."

Alec acknowledged his statement and pronounced, "We'd better let you rest. I understand Dr. Abbot is keeping you here overnight and plans to discharge you in the morning as long as you remain stable."

Yawning, Weissman lowered the back of the bed and said, "Please let the others know I have no idea who killed Sloane. I feel like a sitting duck. I hope you find the guilty party soon. I don't want to keep looking over my shoulder."

Alec understood his sentiments and promised to stay vigilant.

When he and Paige stepped out of the room, Douglas remarked, "Captain Stewart stopped by while you were visiting Mr. Weissman. I updated him on his condition, and he's anxious for you to get to the bottom of this sooner than later!"

Alec nodded miserably.

CHAPTER FIFTEEN

▼

"Spinning Wheel"
Words & Music by David Clayton Thomas
Genre: Psychedelic Rock, Released: May 1969

Tuesday Morning—13th of February
After a sleepless night, Alec hurriedly showered and dressed. He had a million thoughts spinning around in his head and needed to write down what he knew about each suspect. Deciding to make a list, he headed to his office.

Alec was glad that Regina was elsewhere so he could begin his task right away. Starting with a blank word document on his computer, he wrote,

Aaron Sloane's Family and Acquaintances

Victor Bristow
Wife (Laura) had liaison with Aaron Sloane twenty-five years ago
Family vacationed with Aaron and Lena (deceased wife)
Confirmed he's Jen's father through DNA
Had an affair with Lena (ended six months before her death)

Admitted to loving Lena and kept it from his wife
Could have fathered Lena's unborn baby
Daughter (Jennifer) will inherit a 50% share of Sloane's estate
Did not like Aaron Sloane (found him arrogant)

Jennifer Bristow
Disliked Sloane (found him creepy)
Did not know about parent's previous affairs
Did not know Aaron considered her his "daughter"
On the El Caño dig when Lena was bitten by a snake
Will inherit a 50% share of Sloane's estate

Laura Bristow (wife of Victor)
Had an affair with Aaron Sloane twenty-five years ago
Family vacationed with Aaron and Lena
Knew Sloane believed that Jen was his daughter
Suffers with crippling arthritis and is housebound
An archaeologist, now writing a children's book
May or may not have known about Victor's affair with Lena

Michael Donovan
Worked for Aaron Sloane as underwater archaeologist
Obtained notoriety from some of Sloane's discoveries
Knew Lena and had kept his distance from her
Romantically interested in Jennifer Bristow
May benefit from Jen's inheritance

Marshall Weissman
Worked for Aaron Sloane as technology expert
Felt Sloane was not a good husband
Had a brief affair with Lena prior to her death
May have asked Panamanian police to look into Lena's death
Confirmed that Lena was pregnant (possibly with his baby)
May know who killed Aaron Sloane
Accidentally or purposely drugged with fentanyl

Emily Irving
Had been on several digs with Captain Stewart in the past
Argued with Sloane over biblical vs historical archaeology
Went to college with Lena and tried to help her regarding loss of son
Confirmed Lena was happy about pregnancy before she died
Exhibiting new relationship with Charles Stewart

Annette Perkins
Disliked Sloane's personality
Took over from Sloane as president of FAO
Booked Panama cruise after Sloane suggested it
Accused Sloane of stealing valuable artifacts
Described Lena as talented and promiscuous

Charles Stewart
Was an amateur archaeologist trained by Emily
Has become close to Emily since her arrival on the cruise
Possibly angry at Sloane for the way he treated Emily
Set up the party where Marshall was drugged

Franklin Sloane
Brother of Aaron Sloane
Told Aaron to get a DNA test before leaving money to Jen
Verified that Sloane had an open marriage and loved Laura
Confirmed that he and Jen were to share inheritance
Could have tainted his brother's nasal spray

Lena Sloane
Deceased wife of Aaron Sloane
Previously married and lost child in a pool accident
Celebrity archaeologist famous for appearances on TV
Had affairs with Victor Bristow and Marshall Weissman
Happy to be pregnant with possibly Marshall's child
Died from a snake bite while on a dig in Panama

Alec reviewed the list to make sure all his suspects had motive and opportunity. Assured that they probably knew about Sloane's regular use of nasal spray, Alec asked himself, "Could they have given him a fentanyl-laced bottle of nasal spray prior to his arrival on the ship?"

Since the answer was "yes," the only person Alec could remove from his suspect list was Lena Sloane. There was no way a dead woman could kill anyone.

From reports on the news, Alec knew that it was fairly easy for people to purchase fentanyl illicitly on the street. The drug seemed to be everywhere. Alec marveled that more people weren't murdered by the substance.

Hungry for lunch and annoyed that his list hadn't yielded much, Alec printed it out and set off for the infirmary.

The doctor was just going off duty when Alec arrived. He had released Marshall at 11:00 o'clock and relayed, "He had a good night and showed no ill effects from the fentanyl. Narcan has been instrumental in saving thousands of lives. It's a pity, I wasn't able to administer it to Aaron Sloane before it was too late."

Alec frowned and Douglas observed, "You look like you lost your best friend. What's been going on?"

Still feeling miserable, Alec complained, "I feel like I've been on a merry-go-round. None of my suspects stand out. They all had varying reasons to dislike Sloane. I have no idea which one hated Aaron enough to kill him. My head hasn't stopped spinning."

After uttering those words, Alec sang out,

What goes up must come down
Spinning Wheel got to go around
Talking about your troubles it's a crying sin
Ride a painted pony let the Spinning Wheel spin
You got no money, you got no home
Spinning Wheel all alone
Talking about your troubles and you never learn
Ride a painted pony, let the Spinning Wheel turn

Did you find (the) directing sign on the straight and narrow highway
Would you mind a reflecting sign
Just let it shine within your mind
And show you the colors that are real

Someone is waiting just for you
Spinning Wheel, spinning true
Drop all your troubles on the riverside
Catch a painted pony, let the Spinning Wheel fly

Did you find (the) directing sign on the straight and narrow highway
Would you mind a reflecting sign
Just let it shine within your mind
And show you the colors that are real

Someone is waiting just for you
Spinning Wheel, spinning true
Drop all your troubles on the riverside
Catch a painted pony let the Spinning Wheel fly

Glad that Alec didn't have an audience while he was being serenaded, Douglas suggested. "Let's get you something to eat. You always feel better when you have a full stomach."

Alec couldn't deny it, and the two men headed over to the Lido Deck for some delicatessen sandwiches.

Alec and Douglas finished their meal at one thirty. Since the third and final archaeology talk was going to be held at 2:00 PM in the Starlight Lounge, Alec persuaded Douglas to join him for a second time. The twosome entered the lounge twenty minutes early, and Alec remarked, "I'm glad we got here early. This place is filling up fast."

The upcoming lecture was entitled, "Mankind Through the Ages." Four of the archeologists lined up to speak were not among Alec's suspects. He had spoken to them earlier and had ruled them out. The remaining speaker was Emily Irving.

Alec was not surprised to see the captain seated at the front of the auditorium. As it neared two o'clock, Alec saw the Bristows and Michael Donovan find seats with other FAO members. There was a spotlight centered on the stage's podium and behind it was a large film screen.

A few minutes past the hour, Faith, the cruise director, walked in from the right wing of the stage and announced to the group, "Welcome to our last archaeology talk."

Gazing at the number of people in the audience, she continued, "I'm so glad you've been enjoying our archaeology lectures. Without further ado, let me introduce you to Annette Perkins, the President of the Florida Archaeology Organization."

Annette took the microphone from Faith and said, "This afternoon, five of our FAO members are going to discuss, 'Mankind Through the Ages.' Speaking first is one of our foremost experts on the Neanderthal Man."

An elderly fellow with black spectacles came up to the podium and introduced himself. With a British accent, he explained, "I was on a team that was given special permission to reexamine ten Neanderthal skeletons that were discovered in Shanidar Cave, northern Iraq, in the 1950s.

"Neanderthals are an extinct species of archaic human origin that was replaced by Homo Sapiens or modern man. They emerged about 200,000 years ago and first inhabited Eurasia. They were shorter and broader than us. While you might have been able to beat them on the basketball court, they would have throttled you at an arm wrestle."

Showing a slide of a Neanderthal skull beside a Homo Sapien one, he resumed, "Neanderthals had a wide and flaring nose with large nostrils. Some scientists have hypothesized that this was an adaptation that allowed them to breathe cold air more easily while in frigid European climates. Neanderthals also had protruding brows and weak chins. Their jaws were more developed than ours."

Alec was spellbound after listening to him and seeing slides of the cave, the skeletal remains of its inhabitants, and the tools they left behind. He learned that one of the Neanderthals, known as

Nandy, was between thirty and forty-five years old when he died 35,000 to 65,000 years ago.

Nandy's skeleton showed a fracture to the left side of his face, which had probably left him blind in one eye and deaf. He suffered from a degenerative disease and had two partially healed broken legs and a withered right arm, fractured in several places.

Glad he didn't live in those days, Alec eagerly waited to hear from the second speaker. A middle-aged woman took the microphone and explained, "I'm going to tell you all about Ötzi, the Iceman.

"Unlike Nandy who was a Neanderthal, Ötzi was a modern human that was mummified in ice and lived between 3350 and 3105 BC. He was discovered in 1991 by German tourists who were visiting the Italian Alps and thought they had come upon a recently deceased mountaineer.

"From Ötzi's mummified corpse," she continued, "Scientists know he was five feet three inches, weighed around 110 pounds, and was about forty-five years of age. He had eaten less than two hours before his death of a meal consisting of wheat grains and wild goat. From hair analysis, CT scans, and X-rays, much was discovered about his health."

Alec cringed when he heard that Ötzi had whipworm in his intestines, four cracked ribs, and blackened lungs from fireplace soot. He also had sixty-one tiny tattoos of straight lines, which archaeologists believe were applied to areas of the body that had caused him pain.

Ötzi's cloak was made of woven grass, and the rest of his clothing from the leather of different animals. He had with him a copper axe, a chert-bladed knife, and a quiver of fourteen arrows. On his body was a pouch containing small tools, berries, and mushrooms.

The archaeologist summed up her portion of the lecture by saying, "Ötzi was murdered. An arrowhead lodged in his left shoulder shattered the scapula and damaged his nerves. It's believed he bled to death."

Douglas, who was just as enthralled with the talk, turned to Alec and said, "How would you like to solve *that* murder?"

Alec admitted. "Not much," while waiting for the next speaker to take the microphone. This time a couple came up. Alec had talked to them a few days earlier. They were very pleasant, from St. Augustine, and didn't have much to say about Aaron Sloane or the other members. They were relatively new to the organization.

When they announced that their field was Neolithic settlements, Alec was delighted to hear they were going to tell the audience about Skara Brae. Alec and Paige had been to the site on Orkney Island, in northern Scotland, years ago and found the place fascinating.

The couple explained, "The Neolithic Age or New Stone Age occurred between 10,000 BC and 2200 BC. Skara Brae is a cluster of ten flagstone homes that were occupied roughly between 3180 BC and 2500 BC. The site was uncovered by a severe storm in 1850, but little was done to preserve it then. In 1913, during a single weekend, a group with shovels took away an unknown quantity of artifacts.

"Despite that, we've learned a lot about Neolithic life. The inhabitants were makers and users of grooved ware, a distinctive type of Scottish pottery. They raised cattle and sheep, cultivated barley, and depended upon seafood for nourishment. Their homes were sunken into the ground to provide stability to the walls and to act as insulation against the island's harsh winter."

Alec recalled how the houses had looked. They were about 430 square feet in size with a stone hearth for heating and cooking. The dwelling contained stone built pieces of furniture including cupboards, dressers, seats, bed frames, and waterproof storage boxes. Inhabitants had to enter the house through a low doorway that had a stone slab door. They even had a primitive sewer system with "toilets" that flushed waste through drains and out to the ocean.

The couple showed slides of the site and of artifacts excavated from the grounds. The pictures included awls, needles, knives, beads, axes, shovels, small bowls, and ivory pins. Laughing, the woman added, "Scientists discovered remnants of human fleas in the settlement—the first record of fleas in Europe. The site was abandoned for an unknown reason and is known as the Scottish Pompeii. We urge you to visit it the next time you're in Great Britain."

Alec wondered how the next speaker, Emily Irving, was going to stack up against the others. She looked very professional as she stood by the podium and introduced herself.

Softly, she explained, "I'm a biblical archaeologist and responsible for locating artifacts that corroborate the stories and people recorded in the Old and New Testaments. Today, I want to tell you about a farm that was recently unearthed near Israel's northern Sea of Galilee.

"While installing a water pipe to be used for a desalination project, excavators found a farmstead from 100 BC, frozen in time. The farm was in pristine condition. Archaeologists discovered intact storage jars as well as weaving looms used to produce textiles from sheep and goats. Nearly all the iron tools, including various picks and scythes, were still there along with several dated coins. The foundation and pottery shards under the building were from the tenth and ninth century BC.

"These finds not only provide information about a Galilean's daily life but also presents archaeologists with a mystery. Why did the people suddenly leave the farmstead without their possessions?"

Alec listened keenly as she described what was going on historically under Hasmonean rulers in Judea from 140 BC to 37 BC. At that time, local Jewish traditions were disregarded in favor of Greek and Roman customs. The dating of the farm corresponded to the expansion of the Hasmonean dynasty into the Galilee region.

She went on to say, "It's possible the farmstead was abandoned in response to an imminent invasion. More investigation is needed before definitive conclusions can be drawn."

Upon concluding her lecture, Emily Irving invited the audience to ask the panel questions. The period lasted about fifteen minutes. The questions were just as entertaining as the speakers, and it appeared to Alec that the audience was reluctant to let the archaeologists wrap up.

At the program's completion, Faith reminded the passengers to attend the archaeology trivia contest at 8:00 o'clock. On hearing that, Douglas said, "Let's test our knowledge. Join Regina and me for drinks an hour before the contest. There's no way we can lose."

Alec was surprised to see the reserved doctor so animated and promised to meet up with them. Before going their separate ways, Douglas asked, "What do you plan to do in the meantime?"

Looking like a man on a mission, Alec replied, "I'm going to speak to Jennifer Bristow. She was on the El Caño dig with Lena Sloane. She must know something that will shed light on my investigation."

Moments later, Alec followed the Bristows and Donovan out of the lounge, maintaining an adequate distance from Jennifer.

CHAPTER SIXTEEN

▼

"Witchcraft"
Words & Music by Cy Coleman and Carolyn Leigh
Genre: Traditional Pop, Released: December 1957

Tuesday Evening—13th of February

Alec and Paige arrived at the Explorer's Club a few minutes to seven. Douglas and Regina hailed them from a table in the corner of the lounge. The doctor summoned the bartender to order the DunBartons' usual drinks and then asked, "How did it go with Jennifer Bristow? Was she able to give you any pertinent information?"

Alec pulled out a club chair for Paige before taking a seat, sighing, "Not as much as I'd hoped. I caught up with Ms. Bristow at the Holmes Media Café and bought her an iced mint chip latte. She confirmed that the death of Lena was terrible and admitted to blocking out some of the horrendous details."

Paige, who was hearing it for the first time, inquired, "Do you think she was lying?"

Regina suggested, "It's possible she really forgot the particulars. It was five years ago, and Jen may have gone into shock upon seeing a family friend in pain."

The drinks arrived a moment later. Taking a rather large mouthful of Glenlivet, Alec remarked, "I learned more about the dig. A television producer and a cinematographer from National Geographic were with the archaeology team members when they first arrived at El Caño. They wanted to see whether the location was fitting for their ongoing series starring Lena Sloane.

"The two men remained with the team a few days. Jen mentioned that her fellow students were pretty enamored by their presence while they set up the excavation site. When the producer and his aide departed with the video, the archaeologists got down to business and earnestly began their fieldwork."

Douglas stopped Alec and said, "I bet you can watch Lena's previously aired shows."

Alec smiled. "I'm way ahead of you. After talking to Jen, I went back to my office to see what I could find on the internet. I watched several of her videos on YouTube and, I must say, she was something! She had a quality that made you want to protect and kill her, all at the same time."

Paige teased impishly, "Should I be worried?"

"Though beautiful and bewitching," Alec confessed, "You're the only one for me."

Feeling an uncontrollable urge to sing, Alec crooned,

Those fingers in my hair
That sly come-hither stare
That strips my conscience bare
It's witchcraft

And I've got no defense for it
The heat is too intense for it
What good would common sense for it do?

'Cause it's witchcraft, wicked witchcraft
And although I know It's strictly taboo
When you arouse the need in me
My heart says "Yes, indeed" in me
"Proceed with what you're leadin' me to"

It's such an ancient pitch
But one I wouldn't switch
'Cause there's no nicer witch than you

'Cause it's witchcraft, that crazy witchcraft
And although I know it's strictly taboo
When you arouse the need in me
My heart says "Yes, indeed" in me
"Proceed with what you're leadin' me to"

It's such an ancient pitch
But one I'd never switch
'Cause there's no nicer witch than you

Paige kissed her husband's cheek but warned, "That ditty had better be about me."

Alec agreed wholeheartedly and then resumed. "I learned from Jen that Lena was visibly pregnant on the dig and planned to be back in shape after giving birth. She was very excited about having a child.

"Aaron Sloane was less so. Though he assumed the baby was his, Jen heard them argue one night when they stayed at a local hotel. She couldn't hear everything that was said but was not surprised to see Lena storm out of her room cursing, 'I wish he was dead!'"

Douglas muttered, "Maybe Sloane killed her before she could do away with him?"

Regina agreed, "They certainly made a tumultuous couple."

Nodding, Alec continued, "Two days later, Lena was dead. The only other thing I discovered from Jen is that Lena packed the first aid supplies for the dig and that Aaron *wasn't* supposed to come. He joined the team when he heard the television crew was paying for it, and the dig was to be short and for the purposes of conducting preliminary field research."

"I think" Paige concluded, "You unearthed quite a bit of information."

Alec conceded he had but complained, "It doesn't bring me any closer to naming Sloane's killer. I also need to discover who slipped fentanyl into Weissman's drink."

Douglas, taking a sip of his gin and tonic, remarked, "Marshall recovered after being given one dose of Narcan. Some patients need two or three doses before regaining consciousness. He might have received a smaller amount of fentanyl than Sloane. By choosing a public place where he could get immediate help, it's possible his poisoner just wanted to warn him to keep his mouth shut."

Alec shook his head in agreement. "If Marshall had any idea who did it, I think he would have told me. It's more likely he saw something that didn't register at the time. I'll speak to him later to see if he's remembered anything."

Paige patted Alec's arm. "It's all you can do at the moment."

Their conversation came to a halt when Faith entered the lounge with two of her helpers. Looking around the room, she exclaimed, "My, we do have a good crowd for this evening's quiz!"

Alec had to agree. The Explorer's Club was nearly full, with only a few open seats. While Paige was collecting quiz forms and pencils, Faith added, "The Florida Archaeology Organization will be awarding a wonderful prize to this evening's winners. For this competition, your teams can include six or less people."

On the quiz form, Paige wrote down "The Singing Sleuths" for the team name. She usually reserved the designation for music trivia, in which Alec often came up with song titles and the singers of one-hit wonders.

This time, Alec had to depend upon his memory and that of Dr. Abbot. Hoping that his grey cells weren't going to fail him, Alec gave Douglas one form and held another for himself. Paige's task was to write down the final answers when they agreed and be the intermediary if their responses differed.

Regina laughed after noting how serious the two men were taking the contest and whispered to Paige, "I'm glad it's just a quiz and not a joust during the Middle Ages."

Hearing her, Douglas quick wittedly responded, "The pen is mightier than the sword."

Before Paige could comment, a young couple approached the foursome and said, "We're the Byrds. Can we join your team?" Glad to have more brain power, Alec welcomed them and rustled up two spare chairs.

When everyone was settled, Faith announced, "I'm now going to ask you twenty-five questions, worth four points each. I'll repeat them twice. Write down your responses on the blank quiz form. Before we exchange papers for grading, I'll repeat questions you didn't hear or understand. Answers supplied by the FAO are final. Let's begin now."

Faith read out:

1. What is the name given to material evidence that was left behind by humans called?
2. True or False? The four countries that established colonies in the New World were Spain, Netherlands, England, and Italy.
3. True or False? From skeletal bones, scientists can usually determine the size, weight, age, and sex of the deceased.
4. True or False? Modern man (Homo Sapiens) first appeared on earth 10,000 years ago.
5. True or False? Skara Brae was an Old Stone Age settlement in Scotland.
6. What is the name of individuals who had official sanction from a country to destroy ships, take cargo, and keep some of the plunder?
7. True or False? A group of tourists discovered Nandy, the Neanderthal while hiking.
8. True or False? The Golden Age of Piracy was between 1550 and 1620.
9. Which privateer burned down Panama City in 1668?
10. True or False? Scientists can find archaeology sites by looking for strange changes or patterns in the terrain, trees, or plants.

11. What was the nickname for the pirate Edward Teach?
12. True or False? Paleontologists are not considered archaeologists.
13. What kind of archaeologist is responsible for locating sunken ships?
14. True or False? Historic archeology covers the last 10,000 years.
15. What was discovered in Shanidar Cave in Iraq?
16. True or False? It is acceptable for archaeologists to keep 5% of their finds.
17. True or False? Ötzi, the Iceman, died of natural causes in Italy.
18. True or False? Captain Henry Morgan was hanged in 1690.
19. What kind of archaeologists look for evidence to support historical records in the Bible?
20. True or False? Radio carbon dating only works on items containing carbon and are over 50,000 years old.
21. True or False? The Hasmonean Empire occurred in Spain in AD 500.
22. What is prehistoric archaeology?
23. True or False? Human bones contain potassium.
24. True or False? There are many different ways for archaeologists to date artifacts.
25. What do archaeologists call dried feces found at a dig site?

Before playing the trivia game, Alec felt he had all the answers. Halfway through the quiz, he muttered to the others, "I can't be sure I have the right dates."

Paige, who was depending upon the other five members, whispered, "Just do the best you can."

When Faith completed the quiz, several people in the audience asked her to repeat questions for clarity. At that time, Alec changed his response to question number fourteen and looked up at the other team members for confirmation. The young couple agreed with a nod. Alec was thankful they had joined their group. The fellow had degrees in both anthropology and history and was knowledgeable on the subject of archaeology.

A few moments later, the team exchanged papers with a neighboring table. As Alec checked off the answers of the other team, he asked Paige, "Did we get that one right?"

Alec's concerns were addressed when their quiz paper was returned with three out of the twenty-five marked with an X, coming to a score of 88%. Though Alec wanted to get 100%, he said to the others, "I guess we did pretty well."

Another team managed to get 92% and was awarded a free meal at the Rainbow Grill the following day. Realizing that the fourteenth was Valentine's Day, Alec cursed silently. He rose and apologized to Paige, "I have to send a report to FCL headquarters tonight. Carry on and I'll join you back here in about thirty minutes."

Regina gazed at Alec with a puzzled expression but said nothing. Instead, Douglas ordered a second round of drinks for the remaining five and replied, "We'll be here."

Alec hurried over to The Shops where the ship's luxurious gifts and fine jewelry were sold. There were several men milling about cases of rings, bracelets, and earrings. Alec shuddered at seeing prices in the thousands and finally settled upon a showcase that contained multicolored Murano glass bead necklaces that were moderately priced.

After perusing several, Alec asked the sales associate to show him a polished and marbled necklace that had splashes of bright blue, gold, and green. Even though it was strung together with 18kt gold over sterling silver and not solid gold, he decided it would look great on Paige when she was casually dressed in a sweater and jeans. Alec paid 188.00 dollars using his ship's keycard and had it boxed up with a ribbon.

Feeling satisfied, Alec stopped off at his cabin to put the gift in the top drawer of his night table. He was less happy about his murder investigation. He had a little more than twenty-four hours to solve the murder.

Alec returned to the Explorer's Club and was glad to see that the Byrds were still in attendance and a neat Glenlivet was waiting for him on the table. Since Alec didn't have a chance to chat with the newcomers before the contest, he asked, "Have you had much contact with the archaeologists on the cruise?"

Gemma, the young woman, smiled slyly. "I hope you won't think we had an unfair advantage in answering the quiz questions, but my husband and I stayed at the same hotel as the FAO members prior to the cruise. We're from Georgia and I didn't want to drive all the way to Fort Lauderdale hours before boarding the ship."

Alec nodded, "It's always wise to get to Fort Lauderdale the night before the sailing."

Mark, her husband, added, "We were in the bar of the Harbor Beach Resort when they had a welcome reception. About ten of them were at a table and when I heard they were going to be on our cruise, we went over to say hello. Anthropologists have a lot in common with archaeologists. We also examine cultures to learn what makes humans tick."

Finishing off her gin and tonic, Paige remarked, "The Florida archaeologists are definitely a distinctive group. Did you get along with them?"

"Everyone but one," Gemma replied. "He was very unpleasant and snubbed Mark saying that anthropology wasn't a real science and barely a social science. I'm glad I haven't seen him on this cruise."

Alec, with the hairs on his neck standing on end, inquired, "Was his name Aaron Sloane?"

Mark replied, "I think that was his name. He said he was a former president of the Florida Archaeology Organization. I must agree with Gemma. He was extremely rude and continually sprayed nasal decongestant into his nostrils"

Gemma agreed, "It was pretty disgusting."

Laughing, she added, "Later that night, I saw someone take the bottle off his cocktail table. It served him right!"

Cautiously, Alec asked her who took Sloane's nasal spray.

With clarity, they both described the person perfectly, leaving no doubt who the culprit was. Thrilled to finally have an idea who orchestrated Sloane's murder. Alec swallowed the remaining Scotch in his glass and said, "It was really wonderful meeting you two. Paige and I have to leave now, but I think the police in Florida will want to speak with you before you disembark the ship on Thursday morning."

When Gemma opened her mouth in surprise, Douglas relayed to Alec, "I'll fill them in and get their details for you."

Thankfully, Alec rushed Paige out of the lounge and straight to the security chief's office.

CHAPTER SEVENTEEN

▼

"Three Little Birds"
Words & Music by Bob Marley
Genre: Reggae, Released: September 1980

Wednesday Morning—14th of February

Alec was in great spirits when he awoke at nine o'clock. He felt refreshed and knew exactly how he was going to prove that Marshall Weissman killed Aaron Sloane. After conferring with Security Chief Zuma, the captain, and the Fort Lauderdale homicide detective, Alec had a plan.

Since the Pegasus was going to be in international waters for the entire day, McGill gave Zuma permission to search Weissman's cabin. Though cruise lines always have the right to rummage through a passenger's quarters without a search warrant, Zuma and Stewart wanted to make sure that any evidence collected could be introduced in a court of law.

To get the fentanyl into the small opening of a nasal spray bottle, Weissman may have used a syringe. It's possible he held onto it and was still among his possessions in the cabin he shared with Michael Donovan.

Marshall must have kept enough fentanyl to poison himself at the captain's party and used it to throw suspicion on his fellow

FAO members. He chose the perfect time and place to overdose. In the presence of so many onlookers, he would have felt confident in receiving the antidote in time.

Alec reviewed all this in his mind as he breakfasted on coffee and microwaved French toast and sausages. With sticky fingers from the maple syrup, he showered, shaved, and got ready for the day.

At ten past ten, Alec's cabin phone rang. Zuma was at the other end and said, "We're ready for you now. Marshall Weissman and his roommate, Michael Donovan, just left their cabin for the captain's talk in the Starlight Lounge. The program is going to run from ten thirty to eleven thirty. Meet us in front of Marshall's quarters, Room 6116, and we'll search it together."

After checking that his cell phone was completely charged, Alec headed out the door and took the stairway three stories up. Alec had to wait several minutes for the chief and two guards to arrive. Zuma told his men to stay outside the cabin while he used his security keycard to enter the premises.

Alec followed the security chief into the standard-sized balcony suite. Zuma handed Alec plastic gloves to wear. The pair noted that the room steward had been in earlier to make the beds and place fresh towels in the bathroom.

With the camera on his cell phone, Alec began to take pictures of the toiletries in the bathroom, wondering which man—Marshall or Michael they belonged to, There were several items around the sink and other grooming accessories on the glass shelves to the right and left of the mirror. Included were toothbrushes, toothpaste, mouthwash, deodorant, shaving cream and shavers.

Under the sink, there was a long glass shelf with still more items. There was a leather case, large bottles, and hair brushes that didn't fit elsewhere. Alec photographed a bottle of ibuprofen extra-strength capsules, men's multivitamin gummies, and vitamin D3 rapid-release soft gels. Alec didn't think any of them could contain fentanyl and continued to search.

Eagerly, Alec removed a brown toiletry case. Though it didn't have embossed initials on it, Alec carried the bag into the main room and laid its contents on one of the twin beds. Zuma, who was going through the bedstand closer to the balcony, walked over and asked, "Have you found something?"

Alec didn't reply, engrossed in removing a prescription bottle with Marshall's name on it. Although the bottle was supposed to contain Rosuvastatin Calcium, 5 MG tablets, Alec had doubts. It was the only bottle of pills among hair mousse, cologne, manicure set, and telephone charger.

Behind Alec, the chief of security voiced, "Those pills may contain fentanyl. I take a low dose statin drug for high cholesterol and my pills are much smaller than those."

From his pocket, Zuma removed several opioid test strips he had gotten from Douglas earlier and remarked, "The doctor told me we have to crush the pills on a clean surface and add one teaspoon of water to it. The wavy tip of the strip should then be inserted into the concoction for fifteen seconds and allowed to sit for two to five minutes on a flat surface."

Alec nodded, "I guess we'd better test it now. Except for the couple who saw Weissman take Sloane's nasal spray bottle, we can't be certain he killed Sloane."

Both men looked like they were out of their depth as they walked over to the room's newly filled ice bucket. Alec ground down one of the pills in a glass with the back of the tongs and added a small amount of melted ice. Alec timed the whole procedure aware they were possibly wasting their time.

Within three minutes, they had their result. One red line appeared on the testing strip indicating that the pill contained fentanyl. While Zuma deposited the glass, tong, and test strip in a zipped plastic bag and the bottle of pills in another, Alec continued to search for a syringe.

Even though he didn't find one in the manicure set or any other area, he managed to locate a dog-eared letter from Lena between the pages of an equally old paperback book. The note was dated a few weeks before her death. The creased folds on the paper looked very worn as if it had been opened and closed a hundred times.

It read:

My Darling,

I'm sorry I haven't been in contact with you for a while. I had to do some hard thinking about you and my husband. My relationship with Aaron has been deteriorating over the last few years. I want a divorce and plan to speak to him about it when we're away in Panama.

Since I refused to sign his prenuptial agreement before we married, I'm sure he's going to get angry and belligerent. I'm glad we're not going to be alone. Coming along with us will be a few college students, and a site director and his photographer for an upcoming show I'll be doing on the National Geographic Channel.

I've decided to raise our baby and would like you to be part of his life. I know we haven't spent a great amount of time together but, I feel so comfortable around you. Unlike most men, who have tried to control and use me, you've always accepted me as I am. I know people may talk but I really don't care. You've given me the kind of security I've yearned for all my life.

Please forgive me for the things I said to you when we last parted. I didn't want to give you false hope about our relationship. What started out as a brief affair has become much more important to me.

I'll be back in Florida on February 14th. Please call me after I return and let me know your thoughts.

Your Lena

For a moment, Alec felt terribly sorry for Marshall. He was a nice guy that few men respected in spite of his intelligence. Though he was short in stature and often chattered about nonsense, it must have been horrible for him to lose the love of his life. She had seen behind his flaws and wanted to share her life and that of their child with him. Many would have laughed at the two together.

After realizing that time was slipping away and the captain's talk was nearing its end, Alec bagged up the book and letter. He and Zuma made sure to put everything else back in place and scanned the room before leaving with their bagged evidence. The two security guards stationed at the door confirmed that none of the passengers seemed unduly concerned about their presence in the corridor.

Alec and Zuma then deposited the various pieces of evidence in the security chief's locked office. From there, they made their way to the bridge.

On the way, Alec reasoned that it had been imperative for them to remove the pills and letter from the cabin. There was no telling when Marshall planned to get rid of the evidence. Having fentanyl was not enough to incarcerate him. The police lab would need to confirm that *his* fentanyl pills were responsible for killing Sloane.

Alec also wondered what motivated Marshall to poison his boss. It appeared that they worked well together. There was no proof that Sloane killed his wife or hurried along her death. Why did Marshall wait five full years to avenge Lena's death? Something must have happened recently for him to act.

From Weissman's quarters, Alec and Zuma hurried to the bridge to update Captain Stewart. The two men had to wait about ten minutes for Charles to return from his talk in the Starlight Lounge. Apparently, quite a few "fans" had approached him afterward to ask him more personal questions.

The captain's satisfied smile disappeared when he laid eyes upon Alec and his chief of security. The trio disappeared into the captain's ready room to discuss what to do with Marshall Weissman. There were three possibilities—place him in the ship's brig overnight, lock him in his own cabin, or say nothing and let the police arrest him on American soil the following morning.

Alec voiced, "I think Weissman should be held in the ship's brig. If he's allowed to stay in his own cabin, he may get rid of evidence we were unable to locate. It would also be a big mistake to leave his arrest until the following day. He may learn about it ahead of time and find a way to escape.

The captain saw the wisdom of Alec's remark and asked, "Are you sure that Weissman killed Aaron Sloane? I don't want the cruise line to get sued if you're not positive."

Alec nodded. "I can't be certain until the fentanyl in Weissman's pill bottle is tested by the police lab in Fort Lauderdale. My contact, Dan McGill, told me that the fentanyl in Sloane's nasal spray had impurities. They're like fingerprints and can be matched to the remains in Marshall's iced tea and the pills we found in his toiletry kit."

Captain Stewart, growing more concerned, instructed Alec, "Call Dan McGill now and let me know what he thinks."

Alec removed the cell phone from his pocket. McGill's home and work phone numbers were among his contacts. In minutes, he had Dan on the line and put him on speaker to introduce him to the captain and the security chief.

After learning what Alec and Zuma found in Marshall's shared cabin, McGill agreed with Alec and said, "It would be best for you to put Weissman in the brig and give his roommate another accommodation for the night. I want the cabin sealed until my team and I meet the ship in Port Everglades tomorrow.

"The medical examiner's office plans to collect the corpse and other relevant evidence from your doctor by 10:00 o'clock, and my forensics team will require about four hours to examine Weissman's quarters for items you may have missed."

Pausing a moment, McGill asked Alec, "Have you confronted Weissman yet? Is there any way he might confess?"

Alec replied, "It's possible. Something must have happened recently for him to kill Sloane five years *after* Lena's death . He may want to air out his grievances."

McGill confirmed, "I'll want to take statements from some of the FAO members on board the Pegasus before they go their separate ways. Find a private spot for me and my assistant to hold our interviews."

Alec gazed at Stewart and the captain replied, "You can use the Hudson Room. In the meantime, I'll have Security Chief Zuma pick up Weissman and take him to the ship's brig. What should he be told?"

McGill responded, "Tell him he's being held on suspicion of murder. I don't want him talking to anybody until he's been read his Miranda Rights."

Speaking directly to Alec, McGill added. "Let the FAO members know what has transpired today and schedule meetings with those you previously suspected between 8:00 AM and 11:00 AM tomorrow. I'll see Weissman last."

With that said, Alec got off the phone. Zuma left moments later to find out Marshall's current whereabouts. The captain appeared to be pleased and asked Alec to remain behind.

Showing uncharacteristic warmth, Stewart shook Alec's hand and relayed, "I'm glad you were here to investigate the murder. More importantly, I'm relieved that you cleared Emily Irving's name. Suspicion could have ruined her personal and professional reputation."

Alec nodded and made a quick exit. It was one o'clock in the afternoon, and he had quite a bit to do before he could work on the interview list. The first order of business was to tell Douglas that Sloane's body was going to be picked up in the morning and the second was to have lunch.

No longer feeling stressed, Alec sang out,

"Don't worry about a thing
'Cause every little thing is gonna be alright"
Singing, "Don't worry about a thing
'Cause every little thing is gonna be alright!"

Rise up this morning, smiled with the rising sun

> Three little birds pitch by my doorstep
> Singing sweet songs of melodies pure and true
> Saying, "This is my message to you-ou-ou"
>
> Singing, "Don't worry about a thing
> 'Cause every little thing is gonna be alright"
> Singing, "Don't worry about a thing (Don't worry)
> 'Cause every little thing is gonna be alright!"
>
> Rise up this morning, smiled with the rising sun
> Three little birds pitch by my doorstep
> Singing sweet songs of melodies pure and true
> Saying, "This is my message to you-ou-ou"
>
> Singing, "Don't worry about a thing (Worry about a thing, oh)
> 'Cause every little thing is gonna be alright (Don't worry)
> Singing, "Don't worry about a thing (I won't worry)
> 'Cause every little thing is gonna be alright!"
> Singing, "Don't worry about a thing
> 'Cause every little thing is gonna be alright (I won't worry)
> Singing, "Don't worry about a thing
> 'Cause every little thing is gonna be alright!"
> Singing, "Don't worry about a thing (Don't worry about a thing)
> 'Cause every little thing is gonna be alright

Though three little birds had not pitched on his doorstep, Alec was very thankful that he met two other Byrds at the archaeology contest. They had seen Weissman take Sloane's nasal spray at the Harbor Beach Resort. It remained to be seen why Marshall killed Sloane so long after the love of his life had died.

CHAPTER EIGHTEEN

▼

"My Funny Valentine"
Words & Music by Lorenz Hart and Richard Rodgers
Genre: Jazz Standard, Released: April 1937

Wednesday Evening—14th of February

It was 6:10 PM when Alec and Paige entered the Explorer's Club to attend the FAO's farewell cocktail party. Almost every eye looked up at them as they approached Annette Perkins.

Annette welcomed Paige with an uncharacteristic hug and nearly bowed and scraped when she took Alec's hand. A hush came over the group as Annette announced to her members, "Let's all congratulate Mr. Alec DunBarton for solving the murder of Aaron Sloane."

Alec wasn't surprised that they'd learned about Weissman's arrest. News on the Pegasus aways seemed to travel at lightspeed. Alec had wanted to break the news to them at the party.

Seeing that they already knew, he explained, "Marshall Weissman has been placed in the ship's brig overnight on the suspicion of killing Sloane. Nothing can be proven until the police test the fentanyl that was found in his possession. The police will need to interview Marshall and several other people tomorrow morning before you disembark."

Michael Donovan, who was standing very close to Jen Bristow, spoke up, "I guess I'm one of those persons since I roomed with him."

Alec confirmed, "Yes, the homicide detectives will want to see you along with Jennifer Bristow, Victor Bristow, Annette Perkins, and Emily Irving. We'll be holding interviews in the Hudson Room near the Starlight Lounge to collect your official statements. We hope this won't interfere with your travel plans and we'll do what we can to get you on your way."

Emily voiced, "Can you schedule me early in the morning? I have to catch a plane to Texas at one o'clock."

Alec nodded, "That's not a problem." From a list he had drawn up earlier, he read, "The schedule is as follows:

> 8:00 AM   Jemma & Mark Bryd
> 8:30 AM   Emily Irving
> 9:00 AM   Michael Donovan
> 9:30 AM   Jennifer Bristow
> 10:00 AM Victor Bristow
> 10.30 AM Annette Perkins
> 11:00 AM Marshall Weissman

Since no one complained, Alec resumed, "As an employee with the cruise line, I'd like to thank all of you for *supporting me* in my investigation."

Alec knew he was fibbing and getting information from his suspects had been like pulling teeth. Despite that, Alec mingled with the group. Paige chatted with several FAO members who had booked a future cruise with her.

While yummy appetizers were being passed around, Alec had several drinks. Though he never drank to excess, he had to admit he was feeling very good. It was Valentine's Day and he was married to one of the most beautiful women in the world.

Gazing at Paige from a distance, Alec reminded himself that his gift for her was waiting in their cabin. He had also arranged for room service to deliver a meal of chicken parmesan, pappardelle pasta, salad greens, and crusty rolls to their suite at seven.

At five minutes to the hour, Alec sidled up to Paige and winked, "Let's go back to our cabin. I have a surprise for you."

Paige smiled and replied, "I think I may have celebrated a bit too much. I'm ready to spend a relaxing evening with you."

When the couple walked into their cabin, Paige squealed with delight to see two electric candle lights illuminating the dim room and their dinner laid out on the cocktail table in front of their couch. A bottle of champagne was chilling in a standing ice bucket, and the television set was tuned to a romantic favorites music station.

After removing her shoes, Paige hurried over to the food. Both she and Alec took seats on the couch and raised the silver domes covering the plates. Upon taking her first bites, Paige looked around the room and gushed, "When did you have time to do this? You were so busy earlier."

Alec kissed the top of her head and whispered, "I always have time for you."

At that moment, the music station played, "My Funny Valentine." Unwilling to just listen to it, Alec helped Paige to her feet and said, "Shall we?"

Holding her close, they began to dance and he sang.

Behold the way our fine feathered friend,
His virtue doth parade
Thou knowest not, my dim-witted friend
The picture thou hast made
Thy vacant brow, and thy tousled hair
Conceal thy good intent
Thou noble upright truthful sincere,
And slightly dopey gent

You're my funny valentine,
Sweet comic valentine,
You make me smile with my heart.

> Your looks are laughable, un-photographable,
> Yet, you're my favorite work of art.
>
> Is your figure less than Greek?
> Is your mouth a little weak?
> When you open it to speak, are you smart?
> But, don't change a hair for me
> Not if you care for me.
> Stay little valentine, stay!
> Each day is Valentine's Day
>
> Is your figure less than Greek?
> Is your mouth a little weak?
> When you open it to speak, are you smart?
> But, don't change a hair for me
> Not if you care for me.
> Stay little valentine, stay!
> Each day is Valentine's Day

Though half of their meal was uneaten, Alec and Paige ended up on the bed. It was much later when they reheated the uneaten food in the microwave and hungrily finished it. For dessert, Paige was given her Valentine's gift.

Wearing the necklace and nothing else, Paige curled up beside Alec to sleep.

Alec's phone alarm awakened him at six thirty. He had minutes to shave, dress, and meet Dan McGill, his partner, Rachel Franklin, and the forensics unit. Luckily, Douglas had arrived minutes earlier to welcome the group and was on hand to take the forensics team to the cabin that Weissman shared with Donovan.

While the doctor departed with the scientists, Dan gave Alec a hearty handshake and clapped him on the back. For a few moments, the two men sized each other up. It had been about a year since they were last together. Although McGill's hair was a bit more gray, Alec could see he hadn't lost his edge.

McGill winked, "I see you're still enjoying the ship's cuisine."

Alec scoffed and patted his stomach, "Food helps me think. Be grateful I solved another murder for you!"

As they continued to banter, Alec cast his eyes on Rachel Frankin. She was just as underweight as ever, and Alec felt an immediate urge to fatten her up. Hoping that the dining staff had stocked the Hudson Room with coffee, fruit, and pastries, as instructed, Alec escorted them to the meeting room.

Alec was glad to see it was well stocked. While he and Dan helped themselves to coffee, Rachel set up the audio-visual equipment. Zuma stopped by to hand McGill the evidence bags he had locked in his office and to confirm he planned to bring Marshall to the Hudson Room at ten thirty. He left a security staff member to stand guard in the corridor.

Over the next half hour, Alec brought the two homicide officers up to date and let them know he had scheduled the Byrds interview first. The couple arrived a few minutes early and were introduced to Dan McGill.

Gemma, a fan of murder mystery shows, was ecstatic to be involved in a real-life crime. She and Mark answered all the questions posed by McGill in the same manner they had to Alec earlier. If they hadn't noticed Weissman pocket Sloane's nasal spray bottle, Alec would have never been able to isolate Marshall from his list of suspects.

The Byrds departed after giving Rachel Franklin their contact details, including their physical and email addresses and phone numbers. Moments later, Emily Irving and the captain entered the room. Stewart stayed long enough to thank McGill for his help and said to Emily, "I'll wait for you outside."

McGill didn't have much to say to Irving. He wanted to record her remarks about Aaron and Lena Sloane. Upon being asked whether she ever suspected Marshall of killing Sloane, she replied, "I knew Marshall had strong feelings for Lena and, as I said before, Lena was like a new person when I last spoke to her. She was happy and no longer angry at God. It's just too bad that she and Marshall didn't get a chance to make a go of it."

While giving her closing statement, she added, "I've always wondered whether Sloane had anything to do with Lena's death. He wasn't the kind of man to let his wife divorce him with half of his ill-gotten gains."

When Irving exited the room, Dan commented to Alec, "I can see why you had a problem solving the murder. I would have suspected Irving right off the bat. She couldn't find anything nice to say about the victim."

Alec relayed that Sloane and Irving had disagreements in their approach to archaeology while they waited for Michael Donovan to arrive. He rushed in a few minutes late and apologized, "I had to stop by my old cabin to get a new shirt and my toothbrush. The forensics team was able to grab them for me and requested I come back after this interview to take my fingerprints."

McGill explained that his prints were going to be used for exclusion purposes only and thanked him for his patience. Though Alec didn't think Michael was going to be very helpful in building a case against Marshall, he had to admit he underestimated the archaeologist.

For the record, Donovan stated that Weissman always disliked Sloane for dismissing him and discounting his beliefs. Up till a month ago, Marshall had tried to get along with his boss. His feelings towards Sloane changed after they argued at the last FAO meeting. Michael was unable to find out what caused the rift.

On being asked whether Weissman was capable of killing anybody, Donovan replied, "I wouldn't have thought so. He's always been amiable and little got under his skin. He once told me that he and Lena had a *thing* before she died. I didn't believe him. I couldn't imagine her with a guy like him. I guess I should have taken him more seriously."

Alec could understand how easy it was for Marshall's friends, coworkers, and acquaintances to brush him off. Obviously, Aaron Sloane made that fatal error.

Donovan took off upon giving his contact details to Rachel and was followed in by Jennifer Bristow. The two briefly exchanged words by the door and Alec heard Michael say to Jen, "It wasn't bad. Tell them what they want to know."

Jen took the offered seat and looked at Alec tentatively. She seemed more nervous than she ought to be.

McGill put her at ease by asking her first how she enjoyed the cruise. When she warmed up, he inquired, "What were your feelings toward Aaron Sloane?" Jen had plenty to say about the man, good and bad.

As to her upcoming inheritance, she replied, "It will be nice to have some money. My dad thinks I should speak to a financial advisor and have part of it put into a trust or a scholarship fund for archeology students. I really haven't given it much thought."

Alec found her statement hard to believe. It was possible that her romantic relationship with Michael was uppermost on her mind. Ms. Bristow became more tense when asked whether Sloane could have caused his wife's death by taking too much time in getting Lena medical care.

Turning white, Jen reluctantly offered, "It's possible. When two of the college students carried Lena in from the jungle, Aaron said Lena was being overdramatic. It was only after she passed out, we got him to take her to the hospital. I still don't know why he didn't let me come with them."

Looking miserable, she added, "If I had gone with them, Lena may still be with us."

At that moment, Alec realized that Jen held herself responsible for Lena's death and may consider her inheritance blood money. She left the room looking a bit forlorn.

Victor entered a moment later and gave Alec a look that could kill. Bristow was less talkative than his daughter, and McGill had to strongarm him on several occasions.

After a few exchanges, Victor finally became more glib and shared his thoughts about Sloane and Weissman. On being questioned about Lena, Victor confirmed he had an affair with her prior to her relationship with Marshall. Although he doubted Lena was ever serious about Weissman, he stated that his feelings for her were very real.

Victor was dismissed soon after. Unlike Bristow, Annette Perkins was chatty and in no rush to leave the ship. Her car was in one of the Port Everglades parking garages and she just had a three-hour drive to get home.

When asked whether she noticed Marshall argue with Sloane at her last FAO meeting, she answered, "I didn't see anything, but I recall that Marshall vomited in the parking lot. I asked him if he was okay, and he said something like, 'I will be.' I didn't think much of it."

The detectives thanked her and she hugged Alec before turning to leave, declaring, "I didn't like you much when we first met. But, I'm really thankful you didn't give up and figured out who killed Sloane. The FAO will always be grateful that you cleared the names of our organization's members!"

After she slipped out, McGill joked, "You have a real fan." Getting to a more solemn topic, Dan asked Alec, "Have you spoken to Weissman since he was placed in the ship's brig?"

Alec shook his head in the negative but answered, "The chief of security told me that he didn't say a word. He thinks Marshall was expecting it. Overnight, he was also quiet and only asked for a book."

Dan was about to respond when Zuma entered the Hudson Room with Weissman and one of his security team members. Marshall wasn't handcuffed and took the offered seat in front of the audio-visual equipment.

McGill informed Zuma and the guard to wait outside while Rachel Franklin read to Weissman:

You have the right to remain silent. Anything you say can and will be used against you in a court of law. You have the right to speak to an attorney, and to have an attorney present during any questioning. If you cannot afford a lawyer, one will be provided for you at government expense.

Franklin then asked, "Do you understand those rights as read to you?"

Marshall acknowledged he did and replied, "I want to confess. I killed Aaron Sloane. I took his bottle of nasal spray while we were at the Harbor Beach Resort. That night, I injected several crushed fentanyl tablets into the bottle with a syringe. I gave the bottle back to him on the first night of this cruise. I had hoped he would use it overnight and die alone."

Alec spoke up and said, "We pieced that together. We know Lena Sloane was carrying your baby and she wanted you in their lives. Why did you wait five years to kill Sloane?"

McGill and Alec moved their heads closer to him to hear his soft words. After encouraging Marshall to speak louder, he repeated, "At our last regularly scheduled FAO meeting, Aaron and I talked about the upcoming cruise. He mentioned he was eager to see Panama again and planned to celebrate the anniversary of his wife's death. He said some horrible things about Lena and let it slip that she might have survived had he gotten her to the hospital quicker."

Eagerly, McGill asked, "Did he admit to delaying her medical care on purpose?"

Weissman shuddered, "Not in so many words. But, I could tell by the way his beady little eyes glinted. It was the same way they looked after looting a valuable object from his archaeological finds. Sloane was glad to be rid of Lena and laughed at me when I said we loved each other.

"He called me a deluded fool!"

At the ship's 4:00 o'clock Sail Away Party, Alec and Paige joined Douglas and Regina on the Lido Deck. While new passengers were watching the Fort Lauderdale shoreline grow further away from the ship, the doctor asked how things went with McGill and Franklin.

Alec relayed, "Marshall didn't put up a defense for killing Sloane. He felt his boss deserved everything he got and said he would do it all over again. Marshall also told us that he anonymously told the Panamanian officials that Sloane may have killed Lena. He let it drop when they didn't arrest him. McGill and Franklin left with him at noon. He went with them like a lamb to slaughter."

Douglas remarked, "The medical examiner's officer picked up Sloane's corpse as scheduled, and the forensics team finished their investigation by eleven. They took all of Marshall's belongings with them, and Donovan was able to pack up his clothes in time to catch his plane."

"I wonder," Paige remarked, "If his possessions were coated with fingerprint dust."

Alec added, "I'm sure Jen Bristow will brush everything off. They got very friendly on the cruise. Do you think they're going to see each other when they get back home?"

Paige, always the romantic, protested, "They'd better. Away from the watchful eye of her dad, I'm sure Jen will be able to explore her feelings for him."

Regina argued, "She might not have time. Ms. Bristow is in line to inherit a lot of money from Sloane's estate. I hope she spends it wisely."

Douglas agreed and then said, "I feel sorry for Marshall Weissman. He was a smart fellow but not very intuitive about people."

Regina sighed, "We'll never really know whether Sloane did away with his wife. He was a petty man and I wouldn't have put it past him."

Paige offered, "I think it will always remain a mystery."

Watching the ship's newest passengers enjoy their first day on the cruise, drinking Bahama Mama's and dancing to calypso music, Alec noted, "This last case was difficult for me. I hope the next one will be easier to solve."

Paige gazed at her husband and questioned, "The next one?"

EPILOGUE

▼

Alec and Paige were seated on her brother's porch overlooking McClellan Ranch Preserve in Cupertino, California. Paige spied a deer below and said, "Look. It's eating those purple flowers again."

Alec, who was stuffing his pipe with cherry tobacco, replied, "I'm going to miss this place. It's so peaceful after all the running around we've done."

Paige laughed, "We did a lot. You got to meet my relatives and saw some major attractions in California. I especially enjoyed visiting the wineries, Yosemite National Park, and Death Valley.

"I'm glad," Alec remarked, "that Death Vally was one of our first stops. I heard the temperature climbed to 130 degrees yesterday. I think dry heat is overrated."

From the kitchen, Derek Anderson stepped onto the patio and relayed, "Gail just got Oliver to sleep. When she comes downstairs, do you want to watch a movie on tv or stay out here?"

Paige answered her brother, "It's lovely on the porch and the sun is about to set. Alec and I wouldn't mind remaining outside a little longer. The air is a perfect temperature and the breeze is delightful. Could you refresh our drinks?"

Alec gazed at his wife, thankful she was always cognizant of his needs and wants. Cheerfully, Derek called back, "Another gin and tonic for the lady." Laughing, he added, "Should I bring out Alec's bottle of Glenlivet."

Paige indicated with a hand movement for Derek to leave it in the kitchen and said to Alec, "I can't believe our three-month break is nearly over."

Puffing on his pipe, Alec agreed, "The time went by really fast. Meeting your Aunt Jeanne in Los Angeles and her adult kids in San Diego was also a highlight. Do you think we'll ever get your aunt on a plane or ship?"

Overhearing them, Derek handed his sister the drinks and remarked, "Aunt Jeanne hates to travel. When she visits from LA, she comes up by bus. It takes over seven hours for her to get to San Fransico from Los Angeles."

Gail joined them while Derek was talking and sat down wearily on their outdoor rattan couch. Sighing, she exclaimed, "I sometimes think I'm too old to be a mother. When Oliver starts to walk, he's going to run me ragged."

Alec noted, "He's a fast crawler now. Yesterday, I turned around for a few seconds, and he made it to the baby door at the top of the stairs before I could stop him."

Gail turned on the baby monitor beside the couch, listened for a moment, and said, "I think he's settled down for the night. I'm thrilled Aunt Irena is flying in from Boothbay Harbor, Maine, tomorrow and will be going on the Alaska cruise with us and your dad. Both of them have promised to watch Oliver. Your dad is going to pick Irena up at the San Jose Airport. That airport is less crazy than San Francisco International."

Paige admitted, "I can't wait to see Aunt Irena, too. Last July, Alec and I helped her run her bed and breakfast while she recovered from her ankle injury. And, having her on the family cruise with us in Northern Europe was wonderful."

Taking a seat next to Gail, Derek rejoined, "It seems like a million years ago. I can't wait to go on a second cruise with you guys. It will be nice to relax and not worry about having another family member murdered."

Paige shuddered, "Poor Uncle Gustav. At least, he didn't suffer. I'm sure he would have hated to die slowly from brain cancer. Have you heard from Uncle Stefan since he returned to New York?"

Derek replied, "He sent us a congratulations card and check when Oliver was born. We called to thank him and he seemed okay. He told us that he sometimes gets together with Regina for dinner or to see a show."

Paige nodded, "I bet Aunt Regina likes being wined and dined by Stefan now that he has access to Gustav's cookie business profits."

Speaking of business," Alec asked, "Who's going to take care of your catering company while we're away on the cruise? I understand your latest business venture has become very popular.'

"Yes," Derek agreed. I can't believe how quickly Deliteful Dinners and Desserts has grown. We found the perfect niche for people living and working in our area. Many people nowadays want to lose weight healthfully and don't have time to food shop or prepare meals."

"Currently," Gail added, "We have over fifty families enrolled in our meal plan. Along with our catering business, we've been very busy."

Derek nodded. "A few weeks back, I had to hire a couple of chefs and a delivery driver. In fact, the beef Bourguignon we had for dinner was prepared by one of them. He followed my recipe accurately."

Alec patted his stomach. "It was delicious. I'm afraid I've gained about twenty pounds over the last three months."

Paige retorted, "That's from all the junk food you've snacked on. My brother's entrees have less than five hundred calories, are portion controlled, low in saturated fat and sodium, and contain healthy amounts of fiber."

"Only five hundred calories?" Alec marveled. "I'm sure, I could lose weight on your Deliteful Dinners."

Gail suggested. "If you'd like, Derek and I can help you keep you calorie intake down on our cruise. I crafted the diet and Derek can help you choose the right carbohydrates and protein foods. Though the cruise is just nine days, I'm sure you can drop some weight in that time and also develop better eating habits."

Gazing at his wife, Alec concurred. "That would be a great help."

Concerned that Alec was biting off more than he could chew, Paige warned her brother, "Alec may not want to give up his Scottish whisky."

Derek laughed. "I wouldn't think of depriving him of his native beverage! We can eliminate a dessert in its place."

Since Alec wasn't a slave to his sweet tooth, he readily agreed and asked, "So, who beside us is going to be on the cruise to Alaska?

Gail relayed. "We'll be with the local chapter of the American Catering Association. The leadership decided it would be the perfect way for our members to learn about Pacific Northwest cuisine and to sample Alaskan ingredients. It was just lucky that the cruise ship leaving Seattle on the date we wanted was the Pegasus."

"That was lucky," Paige agreed, "It will be nice to sail with you before returning to our official duties on the Pegasus. I really haven't seen many sights in Alaska. Most of the time, Alec and I are too busy or too tired to go on an excursion."

When the conversation got around to the itinerary, Gail interrupted to ask what stops were included on the cruise.

In response, Alec placed his pipe on an ashtray and took the itinerary out of his pants pocket. After unfolding it, he read,

Pegasus Itinerary

Nine-Day Scenic Alaskan Cruise
Seattle to Seattle

Date	Day	Port of Call	Arrival	Departure
3-Aug	Sun	Seattle, Washington		3:00 PM
3-Aug	Sun	Scenic Cruising Puget Sound		
4-Aug	Mon	At Sea		
5-Aug	Tue	Scenic Cruising Stephens Passage		
5-Aug	Tue	Juneau, Alaska	1:00 PM	9:00 PM
6-Aug	Wed	Skagway, Alaska	7:00 AM	8:00 PM
7-Aug	Thu	Scenic Cruising Endicott Arm/Dawes Glacier		
8-Aug	Fri	Sitka, Alaska	8:00 AM	4:00 PM
9-Aug	Sat	Ketchikan, Alaska	7:00 AM	4:00 PM
10-Aug	Sun	At Sea		1:00 PM
11-Aug	Mon	Victoria, Canada	8:00 PM	11:30 PM
12-Aug	Tues	Seattle, Washington	7:00 AM	

Lightheartedly, Gail acknowledged. "It sounds wonderful. I'm glad we still have five days to get ready and pack. I haven't done anything yet." Speaking to her husband, she resumed, "You'd better get our suitcases down from the attic tomorrow."

Paige reminded, "Don't forget to pack sweaters and a warm jacket."

Alec corrected, "And gloves and a hat. It shouldn't be too cold in August, but we've been there when I could have worn a heavy coat."

Paige laughed, "You resembled Nanook from the North on our first cruise to Alaska."

"I also asked you to marry me on that cruise," Alec added.

Paige winked at her husband and then asked Derek, "Do you have any plans to get together with your fellow caterers before the cruise?"

Grimacing slightly, Derek replied, "Like us, many of them are going to stay at The Warwick Hotel in Seattle two nights before the trip."

Paige, noticing her brother's expression, asked, "You don't seem happy about that."

Gazing at Gail with a helpless look, Derek answered, "I should warn you, several of the caterers don't get along well. Many of us have been trained in different fields of food preparation and have diverse views on the culinary arts. The industry can be competitive and cutthroat. One person in our group reported another member for operating an unlicensed food truck and is also suing his assistant chef for breach of contract."

Paige shivered even though the temperature on the porch had not changed and said, "I had no idea that that caterers could be so ruthless."

Gail nodded in agreement. "When we first started Cupertino Caterers, Derek got into a few squabbles with companies that were already operating in our area."

Even worse," Gail continued, "The person who has caused the most strife in our group just added ready-made dinners to his services. We don't trust him. He's a former bodybuilder and wants to put us out of business by serving protein-rich meals for less money. I hope he behaves himself on the cruise."

Taking a sip of his drink, Alec chortled, "It looks like our cruise to Alaska may be more exciting than I had anticipated."

Paige shivered again.

Answers to the Archaeological Quiz

▼

1. What is the name given to material evidence that was left behind by humans called?
    Artifacts

2. True or False? The four countries that established colonies in the New World were Spain, Netherlands, England, and Italy.
    False. The fourth nation was France, not Italy.

3. True or False? From skeletal bones, scientists can usually determine the size, weight, age, and sex of the deceased.
    True.

4. True or False? Modern man (Homo Sapiens) first appeared on earth 10,000 years ago.
    False. According to historic timelines, modern man first emerged about 250,000 years ago.

5. True or False? Skara Brae was an Old Stone Age settlement.
    False. It was a Neolithic or New Stone Age settlement.

6. What is the name of individuals who had official sanction from a country to destroy ships, take cargo, and keep some of the plunder?
    Privateers

7.   True or False? A group of tourists discovered Nandy, the Neanderthal while hiking.
    False. Ötzi, the iceman, was discovered by German tourists.

8.   True or False? The Golden Age of Piracy was between 1550 to 1620.
    False. It occurred between the 1660s and the 1730s.

9.   Which privateer burned down Panama City in 1668?
    Captain Henry Morgan

10.   True or False? Scientists can find archaeology sites by looking for strange changes or patterns in the terrain, trees, or plants.
    True.

11.   What was the nickname for the pirate Edward Teach?
    Blackbeard

12.   True or False? Paleontologists are not considered archaeologists.
    True. Paleontologists study dinosaur bones and other fossils left from before human habitation.

13.   What kind of archaeologist is responsible for locating sunken ships?
    Underwater archaeologists

14.   True or False? Historic archeology covers the last 10,000 years.
    False. Historic archaeology covers the last 5,000 years.

15.   What was discovered in Shanidar Cave in Iraq?
    Neanderthal skeletons

16. True or False? It is acceptable for archaeologists to keep 5% of their finds.
    False. It is considered looting.

17. True or False? Ötzi died of natural causes in Italy.
    False. Ötzi was murdered.

18. True or False? Captain Henry Morgan was hanged in 1690.
    False. Henry Morgan lived out his days in Port Royal, Jamaica, a rich and respected man.

19. What kind of archaeologists look for evidence to support historical records in the Bible?
    Biblical archaeologists

20. True or False? Radio carbon dating only works on items containing carbon and are over 50,000 years old.
    False. Items must contain carbon and be less than 50,000 years old.

21. True or False? The Hasmonean Empire occurred in Spain in AD 500.
    False. The Hasmonean Empire occurred between 140 BC to 37 BC in Israel.

22. What is prehistoric archaeology?
    It covers the time before written records were kept.

23. True or False? Human bones contain potassium.
    True.

24. True or False? There are different ways for archaeologists to date artifacts.
    True.

25.   What do archaeologists call dried feces found at a dig site?
      Coprolites

Copyright Acknowledgments

▼

Addicted To Love
Words and Music by Robert Palmer
© 1986 Bungalow Music
All Rights Administered by Warner Chappell Music Inc.
All Rights Reserved.
Used by Permission of Alfred Music
Reprinted by Permission of Hal Leonard LLC
Pages 84-85

Another One Bites The Dust
Words and Music by John Deacon
© 1980 Queen Music Ltd.
All Rights for the US and Canada Controlled and Administered by
Beechwood Music Corp.
All Rights for the World (excluding the US and Canada)
Controlled and Administered by EMI Music Publishing Ltd.
All Rights Reserved.
International Copyright Secured.
Used by Permission.
Reprinted by Permission of Hal Leonard LLC
Pages 38-39

Behind Blue Eyes
Words and Music by Pete Townshend
© 1971 Towser Tunes, Inc., Fabulous Music Ltd., and Abkco
Music, Inc.
Copyright Renewed
All Rights for Towser Tunes, Inc.
Administered by Universal Music Careers (BMI)
All Rights Reserved.
Used by Permission.
Reprinted by Permission of Hal Leonard LLC
Pages 30-31

Bungle In The Jungle
Words and Music by Ian Anderson
© 1974 Chrysalis Music Ltd.
All Rights Controlled and Administered by BMG Monarch and
BMG Rights Management US LLC.
International Copyright Secured
All Rights Reserved.
Used by Permission.
Reprinted by Permission of Hal Leonard LLC
Pages 125-126

Everybody Wants To Rule The World
Words and Music by Ian Stanley, Roland Orzabal, and Chris
Hughs
© 1985 EMI Virgin Music Ltd., EMI 10 Music Ltd. and Amuse-
ments Ltd.
All Rights Controlled and Administered in the U.S. and Canada by
EMI Virgin Songs, Inc.
All Rights Controlled and Administered in the World excluding
the U.S. and Canada by EMI Virgin Music Ltd.
All Rights Reserved. International Copyright Secured.
Used by Permission.

Reprinted by Permission of Hal Leonard LLC
Page 21

Honesty
Words and Music by Billy Joel
© 1978 Impulsive Music (ASCAP)
International Copyright Secured
All Rights Reserved
Used by Permission
Reprinted by Permission of Hal Leonard LLC
Pages 130-131

Join Together
Words and Music by Pete Townshend
© 1972 Suolubaf Music, Fabulous Music Ltd., and Abkco Music, Inc.
Copyright Renewed
All Rights for Towser Tunes, Inc.
Administered by Universal Music Careers (BMI)
All Rights Reserved.
Used by Permission.
Reprinted by Permission of Hal Leonard LLC
Pages 14-15

Kokomo
Kokomo from COCKTAIL
Music and Lyrics by John Phillips, Terry Melcher, Mike Love and Scott McKenzie
© 1988 Touchstone Pictures Music & Songs, Inc., Spirit Two Music, Inc., Buena Vista Music Company, Daywin Music, Inc., Clairaudient Music Corporation and Spirit One Music
All Rights Reserved.
Used by Permission.

My Funny Valentine
From the Musical Production *Babes in Arms*
Words by Lorenz Hart
Music by Richard Rodgers
© 1937 (Renewed) by Chappell & Co., Inc.
Rights for the Extended Renewal Term in U.S. controlled by WB
Music Corp. and Williamson Music Co.
All Rights Reserved.
Used by Permission.
Reprinted by Permission of Hal Leonard LLC
Pages 167-168

On And On
Words and Music by Stephen Bishop
© 1976 Stephen Bishop Music
Administered by BMG Rights Management US LLC
Used by Permission
International Copyright Secured
All Rights Reserved
Reprinted by Permission of Hal Leonard LLC
Pages 75-76

Panama
Words and Music by Eddie Van Halen, Alex Van Halen, and
David Lee Roth
© 1983 Diamond Dave Music and Mugambi Publishing
All Rights Administered by Warner Chappell Music Inc.
All Rights Reserved
Used by Permission
Reprinted by Permission of Hal Leonard LLC
Pages 105-106

Spinning Wheel
Words and Music by David Clayton Thomas
© 1968 (Renewed 1996) EMI Blackwood Music Inc. and Bay
Music Ltd.
All Rights Controlled and Administered by EMI Blackwood
Music Inc.
All Rights Reserved
International Copyright Secured
Used by Permission
Reprinted by Permission of Hal Leonard LLC
Pages 141-142

The Caves Of Altamira
Words and Music by Carl Becker and Donald Fagan
© 1976 Red Giant Inc.
Copyright Renewed
All Rights Administered by Universal Music Corp. (ASCAP)
All Rights Reserved.
Used by Permission.
Reprinted by Permission of Hal Leonard LLC
Pages 58-59

Three Little Birds
Words and Music by Bob Marley
© 1980 Fifty-Six Hope Music Limited, Primary Wave Music,
and Blue Mountain Music
All Rights for Primary Wave Music and Blue Mountain Music
Administered by Universal Music Corp.
All Rights Reserved.
Used by Permission.
Reprinted by Permission of Hal Leonard LLC
Pages 163-164